Broken Soul

Keith J. Krompinger

ARCHWAY
PUBLISHING

Archway Publishing books may be ordered through booksellers or by contacting:

Archway Publishing
1663 Liberty Drive
Bloomington, IN 47403
www.archwaypublishing.com
844-669-3957

ISBN: 978-1-6657-4056-2 (sc)
ISBN: 978-1-6657-4059-3 (e)

Library of Congress Control Number: 2023905271

Print information available on the last page.

Archway Publishing rev. date: 03/22/2023

ACKNOWLEDGMENTS

To those who helped along the way. Professor Will Steffan, Amelia Beamer, and everyone at Archway Publishing.

CHAPTER 1

The Demon Within

October 12th, 2010

They were all dead. I dropped down to my knees, drenched in blood. I could hear the demon tear away at my soul. How long can I withstand the rage buried deep within me? I am sure to die on this road. If I am to die, I shall take them all with me.

Monday: 5:00AM

"Amanda!" I screamed, jolting up from the nightmare.

At least, I thought it had been a nightmare. I wished it was only a nightmare. I was awake, remembering the recent weeks, the images that never left my mind for long. I felt as though a dagger punctured my lungs, suffocating me. I could hear my daughter weep in her bedroom across the hall. A daughter should never have to suffer the agony of losing her mother. I can still picture it clearly in my head. Blood was splattered across the walls and the stench of death filtered through my nostrils.

My wife was sprawled out on the kitchen table, naked, with parts of her heart stuffed in her mouth. The sight of her made my arms quiver. Within seconds I vomited on the floor and collapsed down to my knees. My heart took a plunge into darkened water. I covered my eyes as tears poured down my cheeks. Lisa just came home from her friend's party when she saw her mother butchered like an animal. She ran to me and grasped me tight, refusing to let go as she wept. We stayed like this for hours as if time had stopped.

Now I looked at my watch. Twelve hours until the funeral. Nothing in my life will ever be the same again, and it gave me a fearful shiver deep within my spine.

I walked to the bathroom and locked the door. Gazing into the mirror I could see the sickness looking back at me, controlling me. From my ears I could hear Lucifer's voice, encouraging me. The sickness grew and grew, pressing harder against my chest. Distraught and overwhelmed, I violently punched the mirror. Blood trickled down my knuckles as I stared at the shattered glass. From my reflection I saw him in my eyes. One turned red and the other a crimson orange. Then he disappeared, as if just a glimmer. I cleared my head and walked to the night stand. On it was the picture of Amanda and me at our wedding day, the sun gleaming on the roses scattered around the pillars surrounding us. I held it in my hands, trying to find some comfort.

10:00 A.M.

I showered and shaved the best I cared to. The sunglasses would go nicely to cover the eyes. I put on my black suit and tie and headed downstairs to the kitchen. A cold shiver rippled through my skin as I walked through the family room. In the kitchen bottles of beer were scattered on the sink and a box of cigarettes lay on the table.

"Ah fuck it." I grabbed a Sam Adam's from the fridge and took a big sip of it. What fucking harm could it do? I had already lost the woman I loved. I took another sip from the bottle, grasping it tighter. My eyes burned with rage and without even noticing, I threw it against the fridge.

"Dad!" Lisa screamed as she entered the room. I barely looked at her.

"Lisa, I'm sorry. I didn't want you to see that. It's just…"

"Dad, it's ok, I know…..I know. I miss her so much." She cried as she spoke. Noticing this I hugged her tight.

"I know sweetheart, so do I, but I promise you. We will get through this. I will always be there for you."

4:45 P.M.

As we got in the jeep I felt a chill slither up through my spinal column. I was not prepared to talk in front of anyone. My throat was trembling just thinking about it. When we arrived at the cemetery my heart was in disarray, not knowing what the outcome would be. From my window I saw friends and family waiting for my arrival. I got out of the jeep and walked languidly down the grassy aisle until I reached the podium. I gripped the podium tight with my hands as sweat protruded down my face. I tried to open my mouth to talk. I closed my eyes and then opened them. I couldn't move a muscle in my body. I wiped tears away and cleared my throat.

"......To be honest, I didn't come here prepared......There's no amount of words that I can say that will change anything." I paused.

"My wife always had a way of touching my soul; that brought out the best qualities in me. I remember when Lisa was first born, the look on her face and the look on my wife's, showing that same radiance."

I paused and cleared my throat again.

"She was the only one who truly understood me, who knew how to comfort me through the dark times.........I'm..... I'm sorry, I can't do this."

At that moment I shuffled away from the podium toward Amanda's coffin. As I moved closer, rain began to fall from the sky. Once in front of the coffin I stood in silence while letting the rain trickle down my face. I dropped to my knees. Tears coated my cheeks. There was no cure for this, no light at the end of the tunnel, just pitch black. Afterward, I grasped the coffin and kissed the top of it. I rose up and continued down the aisle in search of comfort for this unbearable nightmare within. Suddenly, without notice, even to me, my hand dug into my jacket and pulled out my Glock .42. I pressed the side of the weapon against my head in an effort to counteract the violent noises circling in my brain, but my hatred did not allow me to pull the trigger. I put it away before meeting up with my daughter, surrounded by an eerie silence.

"Listen," I said, "why don't you go with Trisha, get something to eat."

"Dad, what are you...."

"Don't worry about me, trust me." Seeing my growing discomfort my partner, Jamie O'Neil, caught up with me and attempted to break the darkness attached to me.

"Ray…I….." But before she could finish I gave her a look of caution and walked by. I got in my jeep and drove into the abyss, trying to wash out the pain.

—◆—

Jennifer Grayson walked out of the hospital and entered the garage parking lot. Exhausted from a grueling surgery, she couldn't wait to relax and embrace her husband. Her watch read ten-forty five on an eerie night, the clouds bathed in a red haze. It was almost as if an omen had been cast. The garage was nearly deserted. She could hear only the crackling of her high heels each time they touched the pavement.

Just then, she was startled by the slam of a car door in the distance. An overwhelming feeling of dread penetrated her heart. She quickened the pace, almost tripping over her toes. Frantically, she wanted to reach her car and find comfort from this feeling. She saw her salvation ten feet away. Closer and closer she came. Finally, after what felt like an eternity, she reached for her keys and abruptly got in the car. To be safe, she immediately locked the doors and scanned left and right out the windows. After the chaos subsided she took a deep breath. A smirk grazed her face and she felt a bit annoyed. The surgery must have gotten to her, she rationalized. She laughed to herself and started the engine. She found the exit and drove into the night.

It took her a good forty minutes to get home. She pulled into the driveway and parked the car in front of the garage. Dr. Grayson stepped outside and felt the refreshing breeze blow past her face. She unlocked the front door and entered her sanctuary. She removed her jacket, placing it on the kitchen chair and tossed her keys down on the table. Outside, an un-welcomed guest slowly slithered out of the car, gazing at the great beauty before him. He could already picture her heart throbbing in his hand, and watch as her blood trickled down her naked breasts. He had a feverish look in his eyes, wanting to taste her sweet, invigorating blood and smell her silky crimson hair. His favorite part would come when he saw the fear in her eyes, the fear of death. The eyes told the entire story, true horror before the eternal darkness. While this sick illusion was pulsating in his head, Jennifer reached for a can of Nestea out of the refrigerator. She took a long gulp of it and pressed the can against her forehead.

"Honey, I'm home. You wouldn't believe what happened at work today, it was a real nightmare. This seventeen year old boy was in a car accident that fractured his spine, really bad. We were in the emergency room for almost twelve hours. Are you there? Ryan?"

There was a strange silence in the room. She could only hear the echo of her own voice.

"Honey, Hey Ryan, where are you?" Still, no response. Trepidation rippled through her veins for a split second as she walked through the house.

"Calm down girl, he's probably upstairs asleep." She said to herself. She cautiously began her way to the stairs and slowly climbed each rung. As she was closer to the top her eyes turned almost white and her breath, suddenly turned dry. She could smell fresh blood on the carpet and looked in absolute horror what lay before her. Terror seeped through her skin, walking fidgety through the hall. Closer to the bedroom she turned right and saw a huge puddle of blood on the floor and blood splatter on the bathroom mirror. Every vein in her skin stood straight up, willing her to continue towards the bedroom. When she was in front of the bedroom door she could see a bloody hand print on the center of it. She slowly pushed it open, only to see her husband's limp body on the bed and his severed head on the nightstand. Lost in utter shock, she covered her mouth and let out a muffled scream as tears blinded her eyes. Within seconds of seeing her dead husband, all the lights in the house went out. Darkness ensued, leaving Jennifer in a sea of fright. Her breathing remained fast and panicked. The lights turned back on and suddenly she could feel the wet liquid of chloroform touch against her nose and mouth. Her instinct was to violently swing her elbows at her unseen assailant, but no matter how hard she tried to escape his grip was too tight. She couldn't even see the black glove holding the cloth as her eyes began to roll to the back of her head. Moments later her arms went limp and she lost consciousness. The intruder was pleased at what he saw. He picked her up and proceeded to carry her downstairs to the basement.

—⚏—

She lay unconscious on the cold, sterile table. The intruder began to cut away at her shirt, smiling. Each cut revealed her smooth, beautiful skin. So overwhelmed with the scent of her luscious stomach, he started to caress her skin, slowly and delicately. The touch never felt so nostalgic. Once finished with her shirt he was compelled to smell the sweet aroma of her navel. He took a big whiff of it and was submerged in absolute pleasure. After this indulgence he grasped the scissors and cut off her bra, revealing her perfectly rounded breasts. The very sight of them furthered his joy. He began stroking them with much delight before heading down to her pants. This time with more urgency rifling through his veins he furiously ripped through them with ease. His eyes revealed the ravenous glow of an animal as his tongue whipped feverishly against his lips. Without control he licked her legs and abdomen. Knowing that the chloroform would wear off soon, he removed four sets of hand-cuffs from his bag. He intelligently restrained her wrists and ankles to the metal bars holding the platforms together. Jennifer's eyes began to flutter until she could see the back of her assailant's head. She remained frozen and still. Realizing she had awakened, the killer slowly turned around and locked his eyes with hers. His eyes revealed a darkly stare and his face resembled that of a burn victim. She looked on in absolute horror and desperately tried to escape. As she rose up she felt herself shackled down to the table. She screamed at the top of her lungs while the killer merely smiled at her. At that moment he pulled out a large double-edged knife from his bag. The glare of the blade pierced her soul. He moved closer and closer towards her. She could only beg for mercy.

"...No!, please, please! don't kill me, please!......help!........ somebody!" Her words echoed in the room. No one was going to save her. He slowly dragged the knife across her stomach, moving closer to her heart. Her eyes widened with terror as she knew what was about to happen. The knife began to dig into her skin. It was then dragged down to her navel. Darkness overtook her.

—✂—

Time had quickly passed as the day shifted to night. My course was unknown until I came across a seedy bar club, no doubt infested with degenerates and desperate women searching for whatever high they can muster. It wasn't my usual establishment but I didn't bother with my moral values and beliefs for they were all but extinguished. As I emerged from the jeep, I prepared to brace myself for what lurked in this unholy of places. Looking around I knew I didn't belong with the crowd and spotted a vacant seat beside a young woman who looked mildly intoxicated. I abruptly ordered a Sam Adams's with much contempt, I never did like the bar scene. The bartender seemed sanitary enough so at least there are some decent people working among the trash. As I was sipping down my beer I could hear a women's voice in the background.

"Ray McPherson, come here to wash away your guilt? After all, Bruce is dead because of you." Said Rachel McTavern

"*Damn it Rachel!* You always have to bring that up. Yes, ok yes, it's my fault, *all of it!* and I accept that, I'll live with it for the rest of my life, but you know *damn* well, I had no other choice."

"*Bullshit!* You had the shot, and you didn't take it, and my husband is dead because of it."

"No, you wouldn't be here if I did, don't you understand? The risks were just too high, yet I struggle with that choice every day. I should've saw it coming. I hesitated, letting my emotions get in the way. For that I'm sorry."

"I know…I know, but I keep on remembering those days, on that island, that horrible place, what those monsters did to my friends. I know I shouldn't blame you for what happened, but that image of Bruce, it doesn't go away."

"No, not for me either, but its only gotten worse. You remember the man with the scars on his face?" Rachel shuddered.

"How could I not, he gave me the chills." I paused before answering her. She could see the sorrow in my eyes.

"Wait, what about him Ray?"

"My wife, Amanda, she was....she was taken from me, *slaughtered!* It was him, now he goes by the name Desmond Reaper." Tears began to flow from Rachel's eyes.

"Oh my God, Ray...I'm so sorry, why? Why does he torment us? *Bastard.*"

"Rachel, I promise you, with *everything* within me, I will avenge all he has taken from us, Bruce, Amanda. He will *die*. He will die *screaming.*"

We sat in the bar room together with a common bond. We shared a disease that feeds off of hate and retribution, a disease that slowly deteriorates the part of us we hold most sacred, our own conscience, without it we are blind to tyranny. Just then as I was enjoying my beer I noticed to my far right another young woman, who seemed to have a glazed look in her eye. I noticed she was actually beginning to fade in and out of consciousness. I looked past her and saw three lewd individuals smirk and gather around her. Their vulgarity was overwhelming, reminding me of a cretin named Drake Winters who enjoyed sexually raping young women. I could taste their filth grinding in my teeth. I guess I have to make myself known to this scum. Rachel knew what was coming.

"Ah shit, they're fucked now, try not to cripple them too badly."

"Nah, I'm just going to teach them a lesson."

"Which is?"

"Isn't it obvious, that sexual predators serve their time in hell." At that defining moment I put away all my codes as an officer and walked toward them with my hand grasped on the beer bottle. I came up close behind the first one.

"Hey." With full force from my arm I violently crushed the bottle on his scalp, chipping away parts of his skin.

"Mother fucker, you're dead." The fool rushed me in haste. I grabbed his left forearm with both hands and bent it upward that shattered the bone. His scream echoed in my ears. I then without a shred of mercy, kicked him in the knee cap with ferocious velocity that the impact forced him on one knee. Noticing his vulnerable position, I took his broken arm and literally threw him back first into the bar table for that added punishment. Of course his fellow miscreants jumped into the fray. I admired their enthusiasm but questioned their judgment. Round two was simple enough. The second one did not learn from the first one's mistake and found himself back dropped through a glass dining table. I imagined the sting of that must have been excruciating. The final poor soul had the same results. I punched him in the stomach, grabbed his neck and kneed him in the face. The second one came at me again. I decided to fight dirty. I pulled out my shotgun from my jacket and shoved it directly in his mouth. Still anxious he went for his gun.

"*Try it! Come on try it!* See what happens, but I'm warning you, I've had a really, *really* bad day and I *despise* rapists, especially those guided by Drake Winters, the same man whose sole purpose in life is to molest the innocent. See, I want to kill you so bad I can barely contain myself; then again I don't want your death on my conscience. To me, you're nothing but a little shit on a wall, an *annoyance*. There is no sense taking your life, you're not my enemy, you're just child's play. Now, I'm gonna give you two choices. Leave this place and take your buddies to the nearest hospital or tempt fate and receive a *bullet in your brain….your choice!*" The cretins did the smartest thing all night and left with nothing but broken bones. Afterwards, I attended to the woman and offered to take her home. She appreciated the gesture but she planned to stay until her sister could pick her up. As I was walking back to Rachel I noticed that Jamie O'Neil had arrived at the bar with a look of concern. She motioned me to come over.

"You wanna tell me what the hell happened in there?!" Jamie asked sternly.

"What's there to tell? Three scumbags tried to take advantage and rape a young woman, I merely stopped them from hurting her."

"That doesn't make it right."

"*No!* Then you tell me what I should've done. Would you have left her at the mercy of the wolves while they *ravished her?!* I did what was absolutely necessary, I saved that girl's life."

"I'm not going to argue with you. I know the path you're taking and I don't like it."

"So now what, you don't trust me? So quick to judge Jamie, I expected more from you."

"This is different. This is only about doing what you believe is right and not taking into consideration what the law permits."

"*The law is inadequate and broken!* Don't you dare try to lecture me on right and wrong. How does it work when *scum* like Drake Winters get away with murder because he has the connections to the wealthiest syndicate in all of New York? Our ideals about justice are thrown in the garbage; its very meaning has been tainted and ripped apart."

"So you would justify taking the law into your own hands like some sort of vigilante, ignoring all the rules of our society and creating your own version of justice?"

"Look, you don't have to be concerned about me, I was merely doing my job, but that's not the issue..is it Jamie?"

A vision rippled through my head. In it, I stumbled down the empty road, my eyes cloaked by the hooded raincoat. The skies went dark as the cold intensified. The rain fell like piercing needles upon my head. I felt my movement slow down which each falling step as human figures rose up from the ground, bloody and inching towards me. The human figures shifted to hollow faced demons, each reaching out to embrace me. I ignored their transgressions and my eyes burned a searing crimson. I saw only Lucifer, his body strewn with the flesh of damaged souls, his razor tipped horns smoldered with ash, and his eyes blood red. Closer and closer I came until I stood within a few feet of this ultimate evil. At that moment I pulled down my hood and whispered "now." I dropped down to my knees with outstretched arms and opened my mouth. The devil peered down, opened his mouth and spewed out a cloud of smoke that forced its way down my throat. Once swallowed, black ink visible upon my skin, raced through my veins and in through my eyes until they became a hollow black.

"God, do not let him in, give me the strength to refuse him."

The nightmares never go away, they come like waves, crashing against my head. They come so often I can hardly function. The drink barely scratches away the pain, it's more of a poison than a remedy. I spend most days drunk, just crouching in the shower, letting the water fall against my back, not caring about the world. Other days are worse, with a gun in my mouth, wanting so desperately to let go and join my wife in the afterlife.... but Lisa, I can't abandon Lisa, no, that would truly be a selfish act, the cowards way out.

Just when it seems the voices call out to end my life, another buries it deep within me. The voice of the demon pounds against my chest, the call for darkness to engulf me, and strangely enough, to save me. Save me? I think to myself, it is merely a cruel game meant to cripple my enemies. There is no morality or righteousness. It is a fixation, one of unmitigated savagery. Day after day it tries to control me, to push my soul deep into the abyss until it disappears entirely. I've been fighting my best to keep it locked away, searching for any light that still exists. Lisa should be all I need to overcome this, but somehow, she's just become a name to me, only a distraction from the mission. Is vengeance the only solace I have left? It is a constant struggle, the fortitude to resist the devil's temptations. We are taught that when we forgive our enemies, we are above them, without sin. It's when we don't forgive and seek out retribution that we become them. Such a strange notion, why? Are both actions the same? A man who butchers the innocent and takes pleasure in it, bares no resemblance to the righteous man who ends the ladders life. His family? Yes, they have to live without a father or husband, but justice was served regardless. No one else has to suffer his wrath. Maybe though, my definition of justice is a sham. True justice, should be measured by one's conscience.

12:41 A.M.

The psychopath carried her corpse up to the dining room and spread her out on the table. He felt as though the job wasn't complete. He needed to send a message. He removed his knife from his pocket and cut into her leg. He looked towards the wall and came up with the perfect words. Once finished he pulled out his cell phone and dialed the desired number.

12:59 A.M.

"Buzzzzzzz, Buzzzzz." I could hear my cell phone pulsating in my pocket. With concern and caution I took it out, pressing it close to my ear.

"……….Hello." Nothing but static. "Hello, who is this?" Static again before the voice rippled through my ears.

"Ten, now I have ten."

"What are you talking about?"

"Sweet sweet Amanda, so lovely, wasn't she? Her scent, oh I remember, like honey."

Cold anger cut through my face.

"*Mother fucker!!!*"

"Ray, Ray, Ray, please, enough is enough. How many times have we been through this? This obsession of yours, it isn't healthy. You just won't let it go."

"*I'm gonna rip out your fucking heart! You understand me?!*"

"So angry all the time, you've got to learn how to relax. By the way, remember that fine piece of meat? What was her name? You know, that hot doctor chick you know. I think I'll pay her a visit."

"If you even *touch her!*" Click. The phone disconnected. "*Shit!*" I instantaneously dialed for back up. The phone started to ring.

"Come on, come on, come on."

"Ray, what the fuck is going on?"

"It's Jennifer, she's in danger." The receiver picked up.

"Ray?" Officer Davidson asked. Abruptly, I answered.

"Jay, get Douglas and Sheffield. Meet me at 103 Westchester Avenue, double time it, a friend of mine is in trouble."

"Fuck, that's Jennifer's house."

"Just get the fuck over there!" Enthusiastically I rushed to the jeep while Jamie followed me. I drove heatedly to the address. Driving at this speed it would take at least twenty-five minutes to get there, too fucking late. Scenario's rifled through my head, trying to force out the worst possible outcome. I knew It was going to be bad, really bad. I pressed harder on the accelerator, weaving and dodging vehicles left and right.

1:26 A.M.

As we neared Jennifer's house I could already see the other squad cars with their strobe lights beaming into my face. There was no hope here, only the bleak color of despair. I stopped forcefully and shot out of the jeep as if possessed. I ran for the house. Jay grabbed me, blocking my path.

"No! You don't want to do this, there's nothing for you in there."

I fought with him on the issue.

"Let go of me! Jen ..... Jen! Let go of me!" I physically tore my way through him and slammed open the door. I immediately fell to my knees when I saw her. She was sprawled out on the dining table with parts of her heart in her mouth, motionless, like a rag doll. Blood was still dripping from her body, her eyes, nothing but white.

"Fuck!" This isn't happening." I pulled on my hair with both hands. "Mother fucker, you mother fucker." Jamie went in after me and looked in shock. She couldn't handle the sight of her as she hurried out the door and vomited on the grass. She interlocked her hands and wrapped them behind her neck. Tears fell from her eyes.

"God, why?" She whispered to herself. Somehow, God was blind to these events, unable to intervene.

I stayed there kneeling, but felt my eyes turn slightly to the left. There I saw it, every word written in blood, every *fucking* one of them.

(TOO LATE, SEE YOU AT ANOTHER FUNERAL.)

Fire ricocheted through every molecule in my body. At that moment I was approached by Officer Davidson.

"Hey, there's something you have to see. It seems like Jen wasn't the only victim." I kept silent, down on my knees.

"Hey, Ray, are you alright?" Without looking in his eyes I spoke.

"No, no I'm not. Show me the body."

With that we both ascended the stairs to the blood stained hallway. I entered the bedroom where Tracy Douglas and Mike Sheffield were looking over the body; the sight sickened my stomach.

"Ray, as you can see it wasn't pretty. He chopped off his damn head, and that's after he gutted him." Mike said.

"So as far as we know, he wanted to make him suffer. Any signs of a struggle?"

"No, he must have caught him off guard. See this puncture mark in his ribcage?" Tracy asked.

"It's too large for a knife. I'm thinking it was a machete of some type."

"Try a sword. I'd say given the tearing and massive blood loss, probably a Katana blade."

"Great, so our friend Desmond Reaper took up swordplay as a hobby. I wouldn't mind spilling his guts with that thing." I replied angrily.

"Man, you've got issues, not to say you're not entitled to them." Tracy said.

I looked at her coldly.

"You're god damn right I do. Do me a favor, cut the bullshit."

"Whoa, hey, come on man, that wasn't necessary." said Mike.

"Don't tell me what isn't necessary Mike, I'll deem that myself. Just tell me if we have any promising leads at this point. I'd like to start winning for a change."

"Unfortunately, the killer was smart, he used hydrogen peroxide to erase any signs of DNA."

"Great, so in other words, we have jack shit, and the more time we waste another victim is being butchered as we speak."

"Hey, look, you have to calm down."

"Don't fucking tell me to calm down! I'm getting sick and tired of this shit! Jamie! Come on, we have work to do."

Jamie looked at me exhausted.

"Ray, I think maybe, we should just continue this in the afternoon. It's too much for me right now. You should get some sleep too."

"Fine, do what you want."

3:30 A.M.

As I parted with Jamie, I decided to pay a visit to a liquor shop in an effort to ease my pain. I left the place with about six bottles of Kailua, Vodka, and some half and half. I arrived home at around 3:45 and drank till I eventually passed out on the couch. Not really a wise idea at all.

Luckily for me, Lisa didn't hear me come in. A note was stuck to the fridge that read: "Reminder, concert at 8." I completely forgot about it too, and she would feel awful performing without her mother there to support her. Something tells me I'll have to take a rain check on that engagement; there was too much work that had to be done. As long as I was doing that the safer she'd be. Still, what kind of father wouldn't have the decency to support his own daughter? I had promised her that I would attend, no matter what the circumstance.

As I blacked out I dreamt I was alone with Amanda. We slowly began to make love. We lay on the bed and kissed through the night, it seemed so romantic and peaceful. Then it stopped, and suddenly as I turned my wife over I realized I had a mouthful of blood. I became terrified at what I saw. I quickly looked to my left and saw my daughter walking toward me, drenched in blood and melting away. At that moment I jolted upward and let out a faint scream. I started to lose my breath. For a minute I felt as motionless as a dead weight. What must I do to alleviate this pain, this horrendous and sickening pain? It was almost like drowning over and over again. I then lay back down and forced myself to sleep through it.

11:45 A.M.

My eyes became blurred by the hangover. I could barely see what was in front of me. Suddenly, I could hear the sound of my cell phone ringing, uncomfortably through my ears. Groggily I pressed on the send button.

"Hello."

"Ray, I've been trying to reach you man, turn on your T.V. channel eight." Jamie answered.

"Ok, hold on." I turned on the TV and switched to the channel.

["Top story, serial rapist Drake Winters broke out of prison by an unknown source early morning at around 3:15. Six guards were found dead and ten wounded at 7:30 A.M. according to Warden Williamson. Evidence suggests that the assailants gained entry from underneath the shower room with high powered explosives. Warden Williamson has assured us that as we speak, local law enforcement has been dispatched to find Drake Winters and his known associates. If anyone sees Winters retreat to a safe area and do not engage him. Convict is considered armed and extremely dangerous."] "Fuck, I think we all know who's behind this."

"How do you want to play it?" asked Jamie.

"Mark Wallace." I said.

"Mark Wallace?"

"I figure two minds alike would share the same hunting grounds. First, it's time to do some "hunting" of our own."

"Are you coming in?" Jamie asked.

"I'll be there in twenty minutes, shit, make that thirty."

"You sure you're alright?"

"Yeah, just a headache, don't ask." My head was still ringing when I got up from the couch. "Ok, time to get focused, even if I do feel like shit." There was work to be done, and people to kill.

12:15 P.M.

I arrived at the office, wearing my black suit and wrinkled red tie that usually meant a big case was afoot. I hadn't shaved for the occasion but hey, fighting crime is an ugly business, cold and dicey. I took out my cigarette and lit it up. I could see Jamie in the conference room waiting for me.

"Hey, there's no smoking in here, you know that." said Officer Sheffield. I shrugged him off.

"So sue me." I opened the door and took a seat next to Jamie. Chief Riley was present as well.

"Chief, Jamie." I acknowledged.

"Ray, for God's sake, do you have to smoke that in here?" Chief Riley asked.

"It's a free country isn't it?"

The Chief gave me a stern look.

"Eh fuck it right? This shit will kill me anyway." I put out the cig and listened in.

"Thank you, ok, let's get right down to it. I don't know how to put this Ray, I know your instinct would be to go after Mark Wallace, but that's simply not an option at this point."

"Sir, Mark Wallace is a key member of the Poison Heart Death Cult. The man's main revenue is drugs and prostitution, not to mention murder." I responded in protest.

"Based on what? We have no substantial evidence to charge him with any of that. Have you forgotten that Mark Wallace has charity organizations all over the city? He's viewed as a fucking humanitarian for Christ's sake."

"*Oh don't give me that shit!* The man is no more a humanitarian that Adolf *fucking* Hitler. Countless women have been cut to pieces by that madman, *raped and burned!*"

"Ray, you know damn well he's good at covering his tracks. In each one of those murders the remains were so charred that finger prints were impossible to detect. We have to let him be for the time being."

"*Chief!*"

"That's an order! End of discussion, under no circumstances are you to engage Wallace. Failure to comply with that is grounds for insubordination."

"Come on Chief, we can bend the rules a little bit…" Jamie stated.

"Look, I know how you must be feeling, but there's nothing I can do about this. Any attempt to confront him and his lawyer's would be all over it."

I looked at him angrily before responding.

"With all due respect Sir, you can go *fuck* yourself." I got up and forcefully exited the room.

———※———

I was used to the nightmares of the cold, black, darkness, it became a constant image. This time, however, I stood in the middle of a dark room with two vertical windows on either side. Whispers began to flow freely back and forth, Amanda, it was Amanda, and the same words, the same exact words. They were too overbearing to hear. Failure and murderer, pounding my head like stones. Suddenly it stopped and then a long silence. The silence was followed by the breaking of glass windows and the slow, bone-chilling flow of blood pouring into the room. My eyes locked in horror and my breath, dry. The blood continued to rise and rise until it covered me completely. I desperately tried to claw my way out. Then like the sound of a hammer striking steel it stopped and I opened my eyes to reality. This feeling crushed my soul further into the abyss, shattering my heart in two. Inside I tried to fight her words, forsake their accusations. Am I really the cause of all this? I refused to believe it. This poison eats away at my very existence and it won't stop until all that's left are ashes.

12:35 P.M.

Lisa walked through the halls of NYU, numb to her surroundings. The barrage of "sorry for your loss" and "It'll be ok" did nothing to ease her state of mind. All it did was provide false hopes in a very much twisted reality. Every now and then she could smell blood and oil that ripped through her soul. Amidst all the pain she was experiencing she questioned her judgment. Why would she agree to perform on this day, only three weeks after her mother's death? Lisa was majoring in music and was the lead cellist in a student ensemble. She even asked her father to attend.

This was not a question of encouragement, as he was going after the man responsible for her mother's death and bringing him to justice.

"Lisa! Over here." The voice projecting in her ear was Lynn Sinclair, fellow cellist and best friend. Lisa lost her current thought and focused on her interrupter.

"Lynn, what's up?"

"Can we talk?"

"What is it Lynn?"

"Look, I know it's been difficult for you, since your mom died but…."

"Believe me, you have no idea."

"Look, I saw the syringe Lisa." Lynn said with much concern.

"Yeah, so….wait, you think I was using?"

"*I saw you Lisa!*"

"Calm down Lynn, I realized how dumb it was and threw it away."

"Don't lie to me, I *fucking* saw you do it."

"What are you, my chaperone? *Mind your damn business!*"

"*No!* It is my business, when my best friend is trying to kill herself, it is my business."

"*Shut up!* You have no idea how it feels to wake up in the middle of the night after seeing your mother *butchered!* And my Dad, the way he reacted, it was like the devil cut out his soul and left him dead. *This; is* the only way to escape the pain."

"There has to be another way Lisa, don't throw your life away, you have to…" Lisa cut her off.

"*What?!* Have to what? Move on with my life? Just forget it ever happened? It doesn't work that way."

"No, look, I just want you to….."

"I know what you're trying to do Lynn, and I appreciate it, but trust me, no one can help me, not even the one person who matters to me the most."

1:26 P.M.

"This is un-*fucking*-believable."

"Ray, you got to stop this." replied Jamie.

"What? What the *fuck* is your problem?"

"What's my problem? You're obsessed with this case. You haven't been sleeping, you come here obviously hung over, and you're fucking smoking again? It's not healthy."

"Really, you've just figured this out now? I mean, did you actually think I would just let this go and forget about the whole thing? I have every *fucking* right to be obsessed."

"*Jesus Ray!* Keep your voice down. Look, I know how you feel but…."

"*No! You don't know how I feel! You couldn't even fathom it!* You're all the same, pretending to know what I'm going through. You know something Jamie, *fuck you!*"

Without hesitation, Jamie immediately slapped me across the face.

"Ray, I…." I just looked at her with poison running through my veins. Rather than say anything I turned my back on her and made my way out of the building. She couldn't say a thing, just stood there motionless.

1:33 P.M.

With this new found poison coursing through my veins, I got in my jeep and drove with a passion. Within twenty minutes I arrived at my house and quickly went upstairs to the attic. Walking up the steel steps I flipped on the switch. The room lit up with the reflection of chrome, revealing my own, personal storage facility. A large rectangular desk was positioned to the right. A mirror was centered on the wall. Amanda always said it reminded her of a secret lab, used for ungodly purposes. If only she knew the truth about this place, and what lies beneath the shadows of my soul. Before sitting down, I looked around and just paused, taking in this surreal moment. I slowly sat down on the chair and pulled it in close. When I gazed into the mirror I saw a flicker of him, menacing, and absolutely euphoric. I peered down at one of the drawers with a haunting smirk on my face. Pulling it back that smirk turned into a cold, calculating stare. In my eyes I could see the blade, a chilling beauty. The razor edged teeth glimmered with unsurpassed brilliance. As I grasped the handle I placed it just in front of my eyes.

The devil looked at me through the blade, enhancing my demon's power, its bloodlust. I could feel every single dose of malice feeding on my soul. The demon was awake; agitate it slight, it will devour everything in its path.

2:17 P.M.

My attention was turned to the large vertical cabinet to my left. I rose up from the chair and walked toward it. I typed in the correct code. As I pulled back the doors I saw her there, in all her magnificence. Her steel handle attached to that beautifully blunt, rectangular mass. I grasped it with both hands, standing it on its handle. Yes, this would be the instrument I'd use tonight. It was the perfect tool for the job, with enough brutality to send a message. At midnight, the serpent's fangs come out to play. Suddenly, I could hear the faint ring of the doorbell from the distance. My instincts told me to put away the sledgehammer and greet the person in need of my attention, no doubt Jamie. Putting the demon aside I reverted back to my normal self. I couldn't give way to my most heinous desires just yet. I walked down the stairs and secured the area. I opened the door and Jamie stood, still with agitation on her face. Before I could generate a response, she opened her mouth.

"Look, can we at least try to work this out? I want to help you through this, as a team; after all, you need me."

I smirked at her.

"Wow, I feel so much better inside, really Jamie, what do you want from me? Do you want me to just do nothing as Reaper's out there killing people? Mark Wallace is in on everything that's happened. I won't stand by and let him get away with this."

"He won't, we just need evidence that's puts him at the crime scene. Without that we have nothing."

"Yeah, so, in other words just let him plan out his next attack on a helpless bystander. Anyway, I already have a way to deal with Mark Wallace."

"What? What aren't you telling me?"

I didn't respond.

"Ray, you are going to tell me the plan right? What happened to working as a team?"

"This isn't your concern Jamie, just let it go."

"I'm worried about you."

"Trust me, you're better off not knowing." If I had told her the truth, what would have stopped her from bringing in the men carrying the straight-jackets? No, for this to be perfect, I needed no interference.

CHAPTER 2
Exquisite Mayhem

November 8th, 2005, 11:23p.m.

I could feel the cold air whistling down my neck, sitting in the cruiser. It was a constant reminder of how much evil has spread through the annals of this once great city. Here I sat, alone, trailing a new menacing threat, a man that can only be described as a monster. Six women had already been taken by this madman, chopped to pieces and burned. Almost given up, I made a last desperate attempt to track him down. Going against all orders, I followed a known associate of his, John Taft, a man with connections to human trafficking. Apparently he made a deal with the NYPD in helping us find and detain Drake Winters. I watched and waited patiently, sipping down my coffee. Suddenly, at that moment, for some inexplicable reason, I felt myself grasp the double barreled shotgun that lay snug between the seats. My mind became lost to me. It was trapped in an empty space. I could only feel the cold.

As if momentarily possessed I opened the door with the shotgun in hand and found myself charging towards the front door. A red haze engulfed my surroundings. I could feel their presence so strongly, their foul aura pulsating through my eyes. It was time to let out some steam. Without thinking rationally, I emphatically kicked down the door, aimed my weapon, and immediately pulled the trigger. The unsuspecting victim could only feel the ferocious impact of the bullet rip through his chest and explode into tiny fragments within his body. He hit the floor hard and brutal. My instincts guided me to the next awaiting victim to my left, who attempted to slash me across the throat with a switchblade. The barrel connected squarely on his forehead before he could make contact. I pulled the trigger.

Brain and blood splattered on my face and his body dropped to the floor. My weapon remained poised and ready for the next encounter. I could hear the clatter of anxiety emanating from the double doors to my left. Anticipating their attack, I wisely pivoted to the left side of the wall. Like desperate wolves they shoved open the doors and started firing without focusing on the target. One of them failed to see me and felt a portion of his skull and brain violently rip out the side of his head. Startled at this sight, the other tried to pin-point his shot but was met with a blistering round to his chest, shattering his spinal column. My eyes remained cold. I took a deep breath and kicked open the doors. What I saw made me want to vomit.

A child's body lay on the table, strangled. How could men commit such evil? My veins burned and my eyes boiled. There was no room for compassion, no room for forgiveness, no room for remorse. Sickened to my stomach I called it in. After I saw the child I could hear movement upstairs. Two people were talking. One I recognized as Taft, the other was Mark Wallace. If only I was fast enough, I could have taken him out right there. With a surge of adrenaline and my eyes pierced with hate I made my way up the stairs.

"Wallaaaaaaaaaaaaaaaace!!!" I yelled into the air. When I came face to face with that slime, predictably he used Taft as a body guard. I looked directly at Taft, who was holding a large machete. At that moment, I dropped the shotgun to the floor.

I slowly revealed my "hunting" knives. It was a fitting counter to the heavy machete. My eyes relished at the encounter when he came barreling towards me. Of course, at the same time Mark had vanished out the fucking window. No matter, all I cared about at the time was annihilating the enemy running towards me. His hands grasped on the handle like a bat, wanting to swing for the fences. He made his move as the blade came down diagonally towards my chest.

Easily, I blocked the blade with my own but the weight was pushing me down. His brute strength guiding the blade, I needed a way to counter the effect. I swung my feet upward until they reached his chest. From this position, I rolled backwards while carrying him with me and abruptly slammed his back and head against the floor.

I coldly allowed him to recover. Finally he threw the machete at me. I was able to dodge it. Seeing the fear in his eyes, I slowly slid my fingers towards the tip of the blades and launched them with pinpoint precision. The blades pierced through his eyes.

2:45 P.M.

"What is it you're not telling me? Jamie asked.

"Nothing, it's just a past memory."

"You're talking about the Hayes case, aren't you?"

"What do you know of it?"

"Only the small details, a boy, Jake Hayes was found dead. You were the investigating Officer. They said it was really bad."

"There was nothing bad about it, more like horrific. What I saw on that day, you could not imagine it. You'd wish it weren't true."

"It was Wallace, wasn't it? You were trailing Mark Wallace."

"John Taft might have done it, but he got his orders from Wallace. I discovered the truth, yet all he got was a slap on the wrist, a free pass, labeled as a fucking humanitarian. They didn't want his reputation to be tainted. Oh, but his judgment will come, sooner than later."

Jamie turned worrisome from the look on my eyes.

"You're gonna kill him aren't you? There has to be more to the story."

"Yes......the boy.......his last name, wasn't Hayes."

"What are you talking about? You said so in your report."

"His name is.......*McPherson*......Jake *McPherson*." The mention of the name startled her.

"Oh my God."

"Yes, he was my son....*They murdered my son!!!* He was at a friend's birthday party, in the park. I wasn't there, I wasn't *fucking* there! I was following up on another case when Mary called me. She told me he just disappeared. One second she saw him, and then he was gone, how does someone *do that!* It had Drake Winters written all over it. That was the time I broke his jaw. He told me…he told me *everything!* about Taft… and Wallace, where they took my son. When I saw him there, strangled on that table, the *rage,* the *uncontrollable rage,* setting my veins on fire. I got my chance. I killed the *bastard* that did it…but not the one who ordered it. All the Chief could say was let it go.…*Let it fucking go!* Wallace had *connections,* the leverage, but I wasn't about to let him slip by me. I followed that *fuck* Taft right to the source, killing *anyone* who got in my way."

"…Ray.…"

"*No!* That man is dead, gone *forever.* My name……..is *Riker,* and at midnight, I'm gonna kill him, and anyone who stands in my way."

"Then you leave me no choice." Jamie took out her cuffs.

"Ray McPherson, you're under arrest."

"Excuse me?"

"For your own safety. Ray, please, turn around and put your hands behind your back."

"You've got to be shitting me, I never expected this from you."

"*Now Ray!, don't test me!*"

"Ok, relax.…" But in the blink of an eye I forced out my sidearm.

"Now that I have your attention, place your weapons on the floor and get down on your knees."

"*Damn it Ray!,* don't do this."

"*Do it Jamie!* I won't ask you again." At first, she didn't budge, so I gave her an incentive by pulling back the loading mechanism. She could tell in my eyes I wasn't joking and complied with my orders.

"Damn you Ray, you're making a terrible mistake."

"Put your hands on top of your head, and don't try anything stupid, I don't want to kill you." I guided her down to the basement.

"I know you want to hate me right now, but trust me, this is for your own good."

"Forgive me if I sound callous, but go to hell, cause that's the only place you're gonna end up if you continue down this path."

"Heh, I'm already there as we speak, I knew this the second God chose to forsake me." Wisely, I removed any item on her that could potentially track me and stepped on them.

"You won't be needing these."

"I'm gonna give you this last chance to reconsider, as a friend, don't do this, I'm begging you."

"I'm sorry Jamie, I truly am, but sometimes you come across a man so evil that even God can't forgive. In those rare cases, it would be a good service to send him rotting into the foul abyss, to never walk this earth ever again."

"*At what cost?* I still believe in you Ray, whether you do or not."

"Such strong conviction Jamie, I hope you're right." With that I locked the coded door.

3:23 P.M.

I made my way back to the attic to plan the attack. I pulled open one of the drawers and removed a large blueprint of Wallace's mansion that I covertly acquired the first time I suspected him. I looked to see which point of entry would benefit me the most. As I scanned it, I came across a glass roof leading down to the second floor. The unexpected charge through the window would be the perfect assault. It would create a vacuum of fear throughout the mansion; maybe in the process innocents could be spared. My intent was to limit the collateral damage; then again, this demon inside me could care less about the backfire. There was no conscience here.

Before committing to the entry point, I had to make sure to take out the guard detail no doubt surrounding the mansion. Knives would handle them, leaving the hammer to the ones inside. The plan was forming nicely. Concealment wasn't an issue, I'm sure the skull mask can provide the necessary scare tactic. Once committed to a set goal, nothing on this earth can prevent it.

5:45P.M.

"Do you think it's wise to show your face here?" Winters asked.

"What exactly are you implying? Do not waste my time with stupid questions." Wallace replied.

"I'm only asking you this because frankly, McPherson…the man is a fucking lunatic."

"You think I don't know that! Idiot! He's the reason I'm having this little gathering. McPherson can't wait for the opportunity to murder me in my sleep and don't think he wouldn't do the same to you. Remember who we answer to. For the glory of Desmond Reaper. Now, get everything ready. I have guests to entertain, and a man to kill."

6:24P.M.

The plan was set, the entry point decided, and the weapons chosen. All that was left was the assault, the sickening and twisted assault. I looked at my watch; it was 6:24 P.M. The day was still young and I had nothing else to go on. Wallace will give me the answers I need. One way or another, I'm going to kill every last one of them. A tide of blood will wash through the city and nothing can stop it. I closed my eyes and went back to the place, the dark place, where Riker was born.

íle de la mort

July 15th, 2000, 11:46 A.M.

She awoke to the sounds of waves rustling in the background, and could feel the crisp air whistle through her crimson hair. She groggily stood up, the wet sand snug between her toes. How had she gotten here? Confusion turned to panic as she gazed upon the debris of the wrecked yacht. Realization kicked in, remembering her friends that accompanied her, no longer together, lost in a void of luscious trees and bush. Stranded from civilization far off the coast of the Caribbean, Reiyiko knew survival hindered upon using her wits and guile. She needed to find her friends and find a way to send for help. She braced herself, stepping carefully through the thicket of green, fear creeping up her spine. Reiyiko could hear the screams and callings of the native wildlife. She continued to walk, trudging deeper in the vast island, utterly defenseless against possible threats. Her eyes were constantly shifting back and forth, mindful of her surroundings. Her eyes were now locked on a strange sight.

Depictions of symbols, as if drawn with white paint, lay visible on every other tree. The symbols revealed a heart shape surrounded by a circle, the heart bleeding past the bottom edge. At that moment Reiyiko shuttered slightly but remained vigilant, trying to wash out the fear the best she could. Scenarios rifled through her brain, there were inhabitants on this island, hospitable or hostile, she could not be certain. All she knew was if there were people here, her friends may still be alive. Still, those images did not give her comfort.

Suddenly, she heard movement from the bushes all around her. Out of the bushes appeared a young man, seemingly eighteen years old. His face and body consumed by white paint, and his eyes cloaked in black. Pieces of bones could be seen in his pierced ears and nose and he wore a belt made of ragged leaves. He stared at Reiyiko, as if studying her. Reiyiko tried to contemplate what he was thinking, but remained cautious.

Just then the young man raised his arm up and signaled her to follow him. He seemed peaceful, yet she was suspicious of a strangers motives. Again, he urged her to follow him.

Though he was frightening in appearance, Reiyiko hesitantly agreed to follow. Perhaps he could guide her to her friends. They walked as if for miles until reaching a clearing. As they reached closer, structures made of wood and stone appeared in front of them. Just then a man donned in red and black paint, abruptly came in front of Reiyiko. This startled her as she gazed upon this bizarre man. The man was intrigued by her appearance. She wore a red crop top torn from the crash, revealing her beautiful toned midriff. Her navy blue shorts accompanied the shirt nicely, and those eyes, an intoxicating jade. Immediately at that moment, her face was bombarded with blue smoke. Her eyes fluttered and she fell into a deep sleep. The man caught her body as she was falling and gently placed her down on the ground. From his pouch, the man removed a small container filled with blood. Looking upon his prey, he saw something unique, a fierceness about her, yet he needed to be sure. He dipped his finger into the blood and drew a line from her forehead down to the bridge of her nose. He drew two additional lines through the center of each eye. Dipping more into the blood, he drew a circle encompassing her navel with two lines on the top and bottom edge, each extending up and down the length of her abdomen. Finally, he placed an image of a heart under her left breast.

The man slowly lifted her up and carried her. He placed her in the center of a large circle outlined in red. Numerous members of the cult emerged to gather around the circle. Two of them entered the circle where Reiyiko was, covered from head to toe in green paint. A horn was blown as the High King emerged from his hut. His head was adorned in a crown made of human bones with a skull placed in the center. White and red paint covered his entire body. He wore a belt made of torn intestine, and over his neck, a necklace with a heart at the center of it. The High King sat upon a stone throne to watch the battle, a battle to the death. Reiyiko began to come to, wondering what had happened. She was led into a trap that she could not foresee. After her eyes adjusted to her environment, she was captivated by the markings on her body. In the blink of an eye, she was hoisted up by one of the green men and felt his fist rain down on her face, sending her crashing back down. She felt the pain intensify as she was kicked hard in the abdomen. She spit out saliva as the crowd erupted in cheers, but the High King remained unamused.

Reiyiko became aware that she was flung into a battle against her will. Before she could react, she was punched in the face again. To the others watching, they saw a weak little girl, afraid and docile. Panic seeped in, as she could feel the man's hands embrace her throat, with full intention of strangling her to death. The other man simply smiled and did nothing, just stood there mocking her.

In that inexplicable moment, Reiyiko had channeled a side of her that had long been dormant. Defenseless and fueled by utter desperation, she grabbed his face with both hands and began pushing her thumbs deep into his eyes with all the strength she could muster. He screamed in utter agony as the crowd let out a gasp of air. Lost in primal rage, Reiyiko jumped upon him and bit into his throat with such ferocity, she ripped out his jugular. The grizzly scene did not seem to faze her. Seeing his brother dead, the second one quickly engaged and drove his knee into her face. She spat out blood from the impact. As she was getting back up, she wiped the blood from her mouth and stared at him with piercing eyes. He rushed toward her like a tiger, but she slid underneath him and bit his ankle. Annoyed, he began striking her in the head multiple times, forcing her to release the grip.

He lifted her up by her hair and thrust his knee into her abdomen, and struck again for good measure. Pain shot up her body and she spat out more blood. She could not match his freakish strength. The man smirked. When he attempted to break her neck, Reiyiko sensed it coming and instinctively went down low, kicking as hard as she could against his groin. This fazed him momentarily so she kicked him again. Now he released his grip on her and dropped down to his knees. Displaying training from her martial arts background, she delivered a bone-jarring roundhouse kick to his face. Then, throwing all caution to the wind, she leapt on top of him and bit a chunk of his nose off, spewing out blood.

The brutality of this fight surprised those watching. They underestimated this petite girl, now shown in the image of a fierce lioness, refusing to give up. The man grabbed at his nose in pain and then felt her hands grasp and push down on his throat, with still strength left within her. With her thumb nails she began to dig into his skin. As his head rose up, she immediately head butted him in the face. Rocked briefly from the impact, Reiyiko had noticed a large stone that lay near the edge of the circle. She quickly grabbed it and lifted it over her foes face, her eyes boiling. Letting out a feral scream she slammed it multiple times on his face, decimating flesh and bone alike. In defiance, she glared at the High King, long and hard.

Looking into her eyes, the High King admired her tenacity. He rose up and gave a signal to his second in command, a man with scars upon his face, his stare menacing. He walked toward Reiyiko and head butted her, knocking her unconscious. As he stared at her body, he knelt down and kissed her navel. In his heart, he had found someone worthy to be by his side, and what a beautiful sight to behold.

July 18th, 2000, 9:23 A.M. McPherson Residence

The early morning sun creaked in through the window pane as I laid asleep with my wife. The scent of her perfume, a peach cream, aroused my senses, gradually making my eyes open. She looked so peaceful as I watched her crimson hair blow slowly from the wind that slipped through the open window. I smiled as I wrapped my arm around her waist. I brushed her hair back softly with my right hand and kissed her delicately on her neck.

"Mmmm" She responded, her eyes still slightly closed. I kissed her on the cheek in response.

"Your aiming is a bit off this morning."

"How silly of me, maybe this will redeem myself." My hand slipped behind her neck and took hold of her shoulder. I pulled her towards me. My lips made contact with hers, holding them there for a good ten seconds. Amanda blushed.

"Heh, you must be in a great mood to kiss me like that, you should do it more often."

"Oh yeah?" I kissed her again. "I can do this all day."

"I certainly hope so Jacky."

"Now we're gonna have some fun." Thinking alike, we pulled the covers over our heads and began to make sweet love. Afterward, I made my way to the shower to prepare for the morning. Much to my delight, Mandy made her presence known alongside me, letting the water pour down our bodies. We kissed again, basking in the pleasure.

"Meet you downstairs honey, I'm gonna make your favorite, sausage and eggs." Mandy said. Mandy got dressed and made her way down to the kitchen. I could smell the coffee from the bedroom. I put on my black suit and made my way down to meet her. I could see my breakfast on the table and my wife dressed in a faded blue crop top and ripped jeans. Her red hair glistening in the sun.

"You're looking sexy today, I like it a lot." She couldn't help herself from smiling.

"Stop looking at me like that, you're making me blush."

"That's the idea, you know you love it."

"You scoundrel! What am I going to do with you?" The morning paper was placed by the coffee table. On the front page a frightening story was being unfolded. Twenty to forty vacationers off the coast of the Caribbean disappeared after venturing far off to a remote island. Some locals were hush when asked about the subject, but others referred to the island in question as île de la mort, translated to "Island of Death." From there the rumors spread, and it was looking more and more to be true. I was enjoying my coffee when my cell phone began to ring.

"Hello."

"Hey man, it's Avery, we got a situation that concerns you."

"What's going on Avery?"

"You know the rumors about íle de la mort right?"

"The island of death? Yeah, wait, you don't think the rumors are true do you?"

"Rachel and Bruce headed down there on a yacht, with Reiyiko and some friends of theirs. Ray, they never made it back. We've been trying to reach them for days now."

Concern raced through my head.

"Fuck, we have to go down there, heard some crazy shit about a group of cannibals or something, real fucked up stuff."

"I'm putting together a rescue team. You were first on the list."

"I'm headed down now, gonna bring Jamie O'Neil, she'll want in on this."

"She was about to be my second choice. Alright, wheels up at eleven hundred. Meet us at the lower conference room."

Mandy realized something was wrong.

"What is it Ray?"

"It's about Bruce and Rachel. They went down to that island. I don't like this, not one bit. Avery is bringing together a special rescue unit."

"Fuck, you be careful down there Ok? Come back to me."

"I have every intention to. Don't worry babe, we're gonna bring them back, that I promise." With that I kissed her on the forehead and headed down to the office.

10:07 A.M. íle de la mort

Reiyiko lay unconscious on a table made of stone. The man with the scarred face was standing next to her. He pulled out a large machete from his belt and began to cut away at her shirt and bra. He smiled when he saw her luscious breasts, warm to the touch. He began stroking them and proceeded to lick her warm nipples. His tongue slithered between her breasts and down her abdomen, he couldn't help himself. The machete then ripped through her shorts, leaving Reiyiko nude. Her bare body was so radiant and beautiful. After this indulgence, he grabbed from the wall a black silk cloth and wrapped it around her breasts, tying it behind her back. Removing a smaller piece of black cloth, he secured it to her waist, making sure to cover up her vagina. After all, no one else should have the right to look upon it, she was his and his alone. Paint was being plastered upon her, a mixture of orange and black, just like the tigers in the wild. A thick black line was drawn across her eyes. He stood back, admiring his work. He took it upon himself to awaken her from her slumber. He gently began to rub smelling salts in front of her nostrils.

Reiyiko shot up from the effect and went to strike at her captor, but he blocked her arm. He looked at her with serene eyes. This took Reiyiko aback. The man began to speak.

"Shhhh, no, no, you are not a prisoner."

"Who are you? Where the fuck are my friends?!" She snapped back.

"No, they are being prepared, they were not worthy."

Reiyiko looked down at her body and anger cut through her eyes.

"What the hell are you doing to me you *perverted fuck?!*"

"Relax my dear, this is the attire of the warrior, ferocious in battle. It suits your soul. You deserve to be praised."

"Answer my question, where are my friends? What did you mean by prepared?"

"Ahh, they are the main course. Their bodies shall provide us with much nourishment."

Reiyiko's skin went cold with fear. She attempted to flee but The Scarred man held her back.

"*What the fuck? Bruce! Rachel!!! Where are you?!!*"

"Nooo, you do not understand, their flesh will make us strong, they will become one with us."

"*No! Fuck you! Amy! Julia!!!*"

The man felt annoyed at this.

"You must be quiet now, shhhh."

Reiyiko immediately punched him in the face, but within seconds, he had his arm wrapped tightly around her neck. He squeezed down hard, cutting off her flow of oxygen.

"Shhhh, go to sleep now, sleeeeeep, I cannot have you like this." Reiyiko briefly murmured something until fading to unconsciousness. The Scarred man kissed her cheek.

"Rest my dear, you will learn in time."

11:00 A.M. J. Edgar Hoover Building (Federal Bureau of Investigation)

I arrived at the conference room ahead of schedule. Avery **"Bone-Crusher"** Jackson was waiting for me with a Dunkin Donuts cold brew just the way I like it, two French vanilla swirls, an oat milk, and the cold foam. He looked at me in amusement, his thick beard and mustache seemingly growing each day. It went well with his bald head. He stood at five feet eleven, jacked up like a machine. He could make even Dwayne Johnson seem small. "Bone-Crusher" seemed the ideal name for such a man, straight from Haiti with an attitude.

"You and your cold foam, what are you, a fucking pussy?"

"Hey fuck you man, that foam really ties the room together, the perfect cherry on top. You just can't recognize the beauty of it."

"Mother fucker please, that's like saying Charlotte Flair is the greatest women's wrestler of all time."

"She *is*, the greatest of all time, are we gonna have this fucking conversation again?"

"Ripley all day."

"Agree to disagree bitch."

"Are you two gonna need a time out? Arguing like a pair of fucking school children." Jamie O'Neil replied, interjecting herself into the conversation.

"Who asked you? We're just having a heathy argument." said Avery.

"Always gotta ruin things by opening your mouth." I replied.

Jamie hit me across the shoulder.

"Some partner you are asshole, we're supposed to have each other's backs."

"Not at this moment **"Blade."** Jamie had her blonde hair in a ponytail. She wore a green crop top and military style BDU's. The resemblance to the Mortal Kombat character Sonya was nearly spot on. In true "Sonya" form she flipped me off and blew me a death kiss.

Next to enter the room was Sam **"Winchester"** Rivers. A man of five foot nine, with tattoos all the way down his arms. One of which was a nineteen sixty seven Chevy Impala, right from the series Supernatural. He even wore the classic plaid button down shirt. A bit of a quiet one but deadly with a Beretta, John Wick deadly. He simply saluted us and took a seat next to Jamie.

"Sup." Laura **"Raven"** McBride replied, entering the room in dark clothing. Her purple hair matched her eye makeup. Her black lips stood out in a crowd. She was a cross between Teen Titan Raven and Gaz from Invader Zim, her midriff slightly exposed with a navel ring.

"Raven, what's up? Been a while, still rocking the depressing black I see." said Sam.

"Heyyy, can't go wrong with that, Raven's a badass." replied Laura.

"That's for sure." I said. Last to enter the room was Mai **"Shell Shock"** Wu Long. The code name "Shell Shock" because she's lethal with a Sai, made famous by the ninja turtle Raphael. Mai was five foot seven with short golden brown hair, wearing a Japanese dojo shirt with a depiction of a dragon at the top corner. It went well with her fire red khakis and samurai sandals. She nodded to everyone and took a seat next to me.

"Alright, everybody settle down. You know why we're all here." Avery tapped on a keyboard and an image of the island projected on the screen.

"íle de la mort" aka Island of Death, located far off the Caribbean in the middle of nowhere. They say a group of cannibals live on that island, devoid of any conscience. Our good friends Bruce and Rachel McTavern were last seen entering the area three days ago, never to return."

"Cannibals huh? Things might get messy down there, no telling what we'll see." Said Mai.

"True, these group of people have their own twisted way of thinking, believe that consuming human flesh will make them stronger, that it somehow replenishes their souls. Really sick stuff." Replied Sam.

"What we know, is their yacht crashed somewhere in the middle of the island. They are out there, alone, with no means to reach out for help. We are going in hot but keep on your toes, watch for any traps, we don't know what to expect down there. They are known to be brutal, with no regard for human decency." said Avery.

"Then we make sure those mother fuckers know, come after our people, they get the hammer. Promise me, whatever happens, we do this together, and if need be, give our lives if it means bringing our people home. Bruce and Rachel are like family to me. Mai, I know Reiyiko is too." Mai gave me an approving look.

"Then it's settled. Everybody gear up. Operation **Spearhead** starts in ten minutes."

11:50 A.M. F.B.I. Armory

I loaded my shotgun and placed it in the holster on my belt. A sledgehammer sat on the bench. Avery raised his eyebrows.

"What's the sledgehammer for?"

"Heh, you never know when you need to get out of a jam, makes sense to use something effective."

"A little dark don't yah think? Hey! I just got the perfect code name for you, Riker! Yeah, Ray **"Riker"** McPherson. What do you think?"

"Actually, sounds pretty damn awesome."

Avery saw in my eyes a slight hint of doubt.

"Hey bro, we will find them and bring em back, ain't no way Bruce is giving up so easily, believe it, and you know Rachel won't either." I gave him a fist bump and walked over to Mai, who was crouched in the corner, twirling her Sai.

"You Ok?" I asked.

She didn't look at me when she answered.

"Reiyiko's not like most girls, she's different."

"I know."

Mai cut me off.

"No, you don't understand, there is darkness within her, a rage, as if primal. If she's backed in a corner she can't restrain herself, always been that way since I met her. I'm just saying she's unpredictable."

"That could be what keeps her alive, given the circumstances."

"I hope you're right, but I have this strange feeling that something terrible will happen."

"Then let it be done to our enemies, whatever the cost."

She looked up at me.

"Whatever the cost." Jamie was sparring by herself with a pair of pristine Katana blades that glimmered with each strike. I came up behind her.

"Maybe we should call you Leonardo instead." She gave me a stern look, but began to smirk."

"Ahhhh, see, you can smile."

"Shut up."

"You ready?" The tension of this mission could be cut with a knife. It was going to get nasty.

"Yeah, better than we were yesterday." She replied, an homage to the great Rock Lee.

"Better than we were yesterday."

PART II

March 12th, 1989

Reiyiko was walking home from school, her head down, lost in thought. She wore a black Metallica shirt with navy blue jeans, ripped as was the style. Her hair was black with various streaks of green to match her eyes. A flat, circular nose ring lay pinched to her left nostril. She was a quiet girl with no friends. Perhaps her appearance displayed that of a loner, which ostracized her from the rest. As a result she had been teased a lot.

One particular group of girls tormented her the most. They ran like a pack, always looking down on others that didn't fit the trend. Carla was the worst, constantly slapping her in the head or tripping her down the hall, causing her books to drop to the floor. Many laughed at her, drawing her ire. Unfortunately she was used to the abuse, especially from her parents, who had treated her less than dirt.

The more abuse she took, the rage inside of her grew. There was one instance when she lashed out at her father, breaking his nose in the process. As much as that might have been satisfying, she ended up in the hospital because of it. He beat her so bad that he cracked her ribs and gave her a black eye to remember her place. He even had the audacity to send her to anger management classes. That was enough to make her leave home. These girls were much tamer though, just irritating, like a nasty house fly. Up to this point, she tried to contain her sporadic fits of rage the best she could, never at all revealing them. Of course they were following her. Their presence felt like a shadow hovering over her. The numbers advantage didn't help matters at all. She could hear them laughing behind her.

"Hey girls, look at this one, what a freak." Carla said.

"Yeah, *wait!* I know what we can do, let's give her a *makeover!*" Denise shouted out. Then like a swarm of cackling hyenas, they pounced, throwing in punches and kicks. For a while she let them pummel her. As she was about to make her move, however, she was surprised that someone came in and ran interference. The girl fending off her attackers was Mai Wu Long. She grabbed Carla by the hair and flung her down to the ground. Seeing an opening, Reiyiko straight kicked Denise in the face and leapt on top of her, reigning down fists. The last girl ran away, soiling herself in the process. Fists kept hammering away at Denise until Mai forcefully grabbed her with both arms and dragged her off.

"*No! That's enough!* You're safe now." Mai said. Despite her words, Reiyiko tried to rush at Denise again. This time Mai held her tighter.

"No, look at me, *look at me!*" Mai turned Reiyiko around, held her face, and looked into her eyes.

"Listen to me, you're ok now, just let it go, it's not worth it." This seemed to settle Reiyiko down as her breathing slowed. She eventually reverted back to normal.

"Thank you. You don't know how much they get under my skin. Sometimes I take things too far, I apologize."

"No need to apologize, I noticed how they've treated you and had to do something. I'm rather new to this school. The name is Mai Wu Long, and you are?"

"Reiyiko, Reiyiko Lee Chang."

"Well Reiyiko, it's nice to have finally met you. I think we will make good friends." From then on they shared a tight bond together, like blood sisters. There was a lot about Reiyiko that Mai admired, especially her courage despite everything she was forced to endure.

One night though in particular, seemed to drastically change everything. It was a stormy night, the rain falling like daggers ricocheting off the windows.

As she lay asleep, Reiyiko was lost in a nightmare. Her entire body was being pulled down by chains that wrapped around her. She tried with all her might to break free, but the chains were too strong. Flames began to rise from the ground and demonic hands reached out and grabbed her arms and legs. She screamed at the top her lungs until several hands gripped at her mouth. As they began pulling her down to a likely hell, she could see her fathers eyes looking back at her. His were hollow.

At that moment she jolted out of her nightmare. Peace though, did not befall upon her. Her reality was looking her straight in the face. Her father stood over her, brandishing a knife. How had he found her here? Shock ran through her veins at first, but her instincts kicked in. When she saw the knife coming at her, she rolled off the bed and grabbed hold of the lamp. He attempted to slash her across the abdomen. She pivoted to her right and smashed the lamp against his head. As he lay slumped over, she immediately grabbed the knife and stabbed him multiple times in the chest which seemed to last for hours. Survival was the only thing that raced through her mind. Serenity did not last long, however, as her mother came up from behind and started to choke her. How horrible it was, that her own parents would wish death upon her.

Reiyiko pushed her mother backward, slamming her back against the wall, again and again, until she got free. Then, with pure animosity, she slammed the back of her mother's head repeatedly against the wall. Blood and brain matter exited out, staining the walls. At that moment, she could see the red and blue lights shine off the windows. It was self-defense, she thought to herself.

Too bad the courts didn't entirely agree with that. Instead of incarcerating her, they sent to her to a psychiatric ward for observation for a while, until they deemed fit to release her back to society. The news of this angered Mai. She constantly visited, vowing one day to set her free. During those visits, however, she noticed a change in Reiyiko's demeanor, she seemed off at times, devoid of much emotion. This worried Mai. The friend that she knew would never be the same again.

île de la mort

The entire cult were seen gathered around in a circle, their stomachs craving delectable meats. These people appeared almost pale in color. They were adorned with long black robes lined at the edge with red lacing. Long wooden tables were lined up on the perimeter of the dining room, with a large serving table positioned in the center. The desperate cries of the people demanding food was deafening. Reiyiko could hear them across the adjacent room. At that moment, The Scarred man forcefully dragged her by the arm to where the others were. He had her draped in a stone crown of her own and was guiding her to a seat next to the High King. Not wanting her to disrespect her hosts, The Scarred man restrained her waist to the chair with a sturdy rope. He couldn't bear to see her try and flee again. At that moment, strange chanting engulfed the room as The Chef appeared, bringing out the main course, a beautiful American girl, twenty-four, by the looks of her. Her name was Julia Burns. She was nude and unconscious as multiple men carried her above their heads. They then placed her on the serving table. Reiyiko's eyes grew wide with shock and horror.

"Nooooo, *Julia!! Get away from her!!*" Reiyiko screamed out. Frantically, she tried to move to get to her, but she was pulled back by the rope.

"*Be silent!* You will learn soon enough." replied The Scarred Man.

The Chef produced a folded up cloth and placed it on the table. He unwrapped the cloth to reveal various carving knives, the blades like razors. Before committing to the meal, he restrained her wrists and ankles to the table with thick ropes. He moved closer to her and took in the scent of her navel. He proceeded to lick every morsel of it. Reiyiko had tears streaming down her eyes. There was nothing she could do to save her friend. She remained paralyzed with dread. Just then The Chef grabbed hold of a knife and slid the side of it down Julia's entire abdomen and up toward her breasts. An eerie grin formed on his mouth. Looking down, he brought the knife to her right ankle. It was time. The blade slowly began to cut through her ankle as her screams echoed throughout the room. The pain was excruciating as the knife continued to cut through flesh and bone. As her foot was completely cut off, blood seeped down the table. The Chef held it in his hand and began sucking away at her sweet toes, saliva soaking in between the crevasses. Before Reiyiko could scream again, The Scarred man secured a cloth across her mouth. Julia felt weaker as her blood continued to flow out. Once done savoring her foot, The Chef tossed it toward a section of the crowd and they swarmed at it like ravenous dogs. Tears flowed down Julia's face. She was lost in hopelessness. The very sight was sickening to Reiyiko, her face ripe with anger and sorrow. Unfortunately, the horror would not stop there.

The Chef picked up the largest knife on the table and didn't waste any time. Before Julia could react, the knife dug violently into her skin, just below her breasts. It was dragged straight down to her navel. She was already dead. Delighted at what he saw, The Chef grabbed her heart and ripped it from her body. Blood dripped down on his face as he began to take bites out of it. The crowd roared with excitement. Afterward, Julia's entire body was served up to the men and women. Her legs, arms, and breasts were cut up to pieces. The Chef saved her torso, however, for The High King and The Scarred Man, even offering Reiyiko a piece.

She threw up in her mouth. As this terrifying sight continued to give her nightmares, she shuttered at what awaited the others. Was there any hope left to lean on? she wondered, with not much optimism.

Further down the underground tunnels, Rachel McTavern was resting in her cage. When she began to awaken, she was startled by the array of human bones and body parts surrounding her. The rot of death assaulted her senses. She screamed at the sight, letting fear consume her.

Her husband, Bruce McTavern rushed to her side.

"Rachel, it's ok, it's me, it's me, shhhhhh. I got you."

Rachel remained in a state of panic, but slowly steadied her breathing, his embrace easing her down.

"Bruce, we have to get out of here, I can't take it anymore."

"I know...I know, try and relax, I know it looks grim, but have faith."

"Faith, *faith!* Julia is *fucking dead!* Those screams, those *horrible* screams, I can't get them out of my *head.* Who's gonna save us?" Bruce took hold of her face with both hands, his face determined.

"Ray, he's coming for us. Avery must have told him we've been missing for days, I have to believe that. You know him, and Jamie. Trust in that, believe in that." At that moment he kissed Rachel on the lips.

"Hold on to hope, I beg of you."

Rachel looked at him with calmer eyes. She took a deep breath.

"Yes, he's coming, he's coming."

2:30 P.M.

The sound of the propellers stormed on through the clouds. Trisha **"Cobra"** Mills was in the cockpit. Her destination was íle de la mort, nearly one in a half hours away. The team were in the cargo bay, silent, focused on the task at hand. They were going in nearly blind, unaware of the horrors they might discover. While confidence was high there still existed a hint of fear. Not fear of death, for they were accustomed to staring it in the face every day, but fear of facing an unfamiliar enemy, of pure barbarism.

Ray McPherson could only think about his friends, wondering how long they could last. He needed to hold on to hope that they weren't walking into a futile battle. His eyes remained cold and dead ahead. Little did he know a beast lay within him. This mission had the power to alter the mind, molding it to a cruel abomination. One and a half hours to go, until hell comes reigning down.

île de la mort

Reiyiko was thrown into a cage of her own. The Scarred Man who originally treated her with such affection, showed a more aggressive side. Perhaps this was his way of toughening her up to the horrors she's seen.

"You will learn your place my vixen. This may seem cruel, but it's necessary to harden your soul. You are not like your friends, you are something more. Can't you see it?"

"Go to hell, I am nothing like you or the people you follow. They butchered my friend in front of me and you *expect sympathy! Fuck you!*"

"*Enough!* Don't pretend anymore. The way you handled yourself in the death pit, you are not human, you are a *savage* animal, strong in spirit. Julia was weak and pitiful. When she was inside the circle, her cowardice shown through, whimpering like a wounded calf lost in the herd. She was unworthy to die as a warrior. Her mind, her body, and soul was devoured as purely sustenance for our family. It was meaningless. *You are better than that!* Know yourself, erase this shell I see before me, embrace the power within you. Imagine it, join us, and bask in all the freedoms we provide. Until then, you shall remain in this cage."

Reiyiko glared at him with piercing eyes before she kicked her cage in fury.

The Scarred Man walked away.

4:15 P.M. île de la mort

The helicopter hovered silently in the air as the team dropped down on the island. The first one down was Jamie, followed by Ray and Sam. A few minutes later Laura, Mai, and Avery followed suit. Each member was in full SWAT gear, though Jamie made some modifications. She made sure to expose her midriff.

"Really?" I stated with a smirk.

"A girl this badass has to look good after all. That's my motto and I'm sticking to it."

"You're hopeless."

"Shut up, deep down, I know you love it sicko."

Avery was annoyed at the conversation.

"*Shut the fuck up!* Stay focused, we have a job to do." With that we settled in, our weapons poised and ready.

The air was hot and damp. They moved, swiftly and silently in single file, down the dirt and muddy pathways. The noises of the wild snuffed out of their minds. As they came closer toward the center of the island, Avery halted the company with a sharp raise of his hand. He had come across a hidden line of rope that was tied to a pair of trees. Looking up at a diagonal angle, he traced the lines up a tree, and a makeshift structure of razor tipped sticks were visible that could have easily skewered a man. The team slowly evaded the trap and ascended up hill and around it. Silence was the only sound emanating around them for several minutes. The island seemed almost abandoned, where were the inhabitants hiding, I thought to myself. An abrupt stop again was issued by Avery as he saw a young man bathed in white paint a few feet away, his back towards them. Avery signaled everyone to take cover. He then motioned for Jamie to come closer.

"Jamie, see that young man over there?" He whispered.

Jamie nodded.

"I don't like this. Who is he? What's he doing here? We haven't seen or heard anyone up until now." Jamie replied.

"Exactly, I want you to engage him, try and get him talking. Raven, head up that cliff with your sniper, watch for any movement in the trees. Shell Shock, Winchester, scan the perimeter on either side, let's see if you can draw any of these bastards out. Riker, with me, covering Blade."

We all nodded in approval. The young man was still clueless to our arrival. Cautiously, Jamie stepped out of her cover and slowly walked toward the young man. The young man, sensing her presence, turned to face her. Immediately, his eyes glowed with euphoria. He saw before him a very attractive woman, but that exposed midriff looked so delicious to him that his mouth started to water inside. Normally he could hold it back and stay focused on the lure, but Jamie was too irresistible. Jamie creaked a smile at him, shading her utter disgust. He started to regain his composure and signaled her to follow him, much like he did with Reiyiko. He relished at the trap he had set on that day. Now was even more exciting. As much as he wanted to grope her body, he wanted even more to see her violated like a whore before consuming her delicious flesh. He knew the man lying in wait would put her to a most beautiful sleep.

Just then, Sam heard a slight scuffle in the bushes far to his left. In a sudden instant, a man armed with a knife was starting to run towards Jamie. She saw him coming from the corner of her eye. Shock overcame her slightly. The green painted man was tall and bulky, approaching her with a savory appetite. Fortunately, Laura had easily spotted him and had a laser site fixed on his cranium. The soft squeeze of the trigger sent the bullet ripping through his skull, exploding off fragments of brain tissue. This startled the young man as he started to run away. At that instant, Jamie pursued after him. At the same time, Sam found his prey lurking in the bushes and dragged him down to the ground before slitting his throat.

More had emerged from their hiding places and engaged in battle. One came at Mai with a knife, attempting to gut her, but he was sloppy, without discipline. Mai evaded the strike and grabbed him by the arm, removing her Sai at the same time. She thrust it underneath his forearm, quickly ripped it out and stabbed him in the eye. Blood streamed out his face as she retracted her weapon. Ray was confronting a man armed with a spear. He lunged the tip of it at him in quick succession, each strike missing the target. Ray pivoted to the left and grabbed the middle of the handle with both hands, before breaking it in half with his knee. He then elbowed his adversary in the face, drawing him back. Rather than reach for his firearm, he produced the sledgehammer from his back holster. The man charged toward him. He was fast, but not fast enough. Ray spun to the side of him and swung the hammer against the back of his head. The force knocked out four of his teeth. When he fell face down on the ground, Ray slammed the hammer on top of his skull again.

Avery was busy with a brute of a man with one eye, who trapped him in a bear hug. Avery withstood the pain before he had enough. He reared back his head and pummeled him hard with a head butt. The force was like a blistering freight train. The impact sent the large man to the ground. It angered Avery, that this asshole actually caused him pain. In a boiling stew of rage, he stormed toward his opponent and grabbed him by the back of the neck. He dragged him to a tree a repeatedly rammed his face into the bark until he turned it to mush.

"*Mother fucker!*" Avery shouted before spitting on him. Jamie kept in pace with the young man, gaining speed. She entered a large open area with several red circles drawn in red paint on the ground. Hesitantly, she stopped her pursuit and examined the markings. After a couple seconds, she felt something pierce her navel. A dart.

"Fuck..." She stated before her eyes became hazy. Darkness enveloped her as she fell unconscious. The young man merely smiled at her, gazing down at her exposed midriff. His favorite victim fell into his trap. He bent down and licked her navel. Five men then gathered around her and began cutting away at her clothing, preparing her for the fight to come.

"Everybody good!? Roll call, Riker?" shouted Avery.

"Here boss." I stated.

"Winchester?"

"All good here." Sam replied.

"Raven?"

"Sup." Laura answered.

"Shell Shock?"

"Still breathing." Mai said.

"Blade?" No answer.

"*Blade?!*" Nothing still.

"Fuck, where the hell is she?" Exclaimed Avery.

"Last I saw she was chasing down the young man." I said.

"Fan out! We're going after her." said Avery. The remainder of the team followed suit, moving with a purpose. Jamie wouldn't have left on her own.

Jamie gradually began to wake from her slumber. She was annoyed that she fell for a such an obvious trap. "Idiot!" She said to herself, now regretting the modifications she made to her attire. She felt uncomfortable, and looked down to find her combat boots, socks, and pants were taken. Instead she had on a makeshift mini skirt made of ragged leaves and feathers, seemingly held together by some sort of crude paste. At least they kept her crop top on, but she was totally stripped of her gear and weapons. She noticed the unusual markings on her body. A circle wrapped around her navel and a line ran underneath her breasts. Below her left breast was an image of a heart, a bit creepy for her tastes. Finally, one thick line was drawn down the bridge of her nose. As she began to rise to her feet she noticed several men and women were gathered around her. She noticed she was in a large circle outlined in red and came to the conclusion that she was entangled in some sort of strange ritual. She soon knew what kind of ritual. Out of the crowd appeared four men covered with green paint from head to toe, followed by a fifth one submerged in red. These men had the physiques of elite athletes, though the one in red seemed the Alpha of the pack. This was to be a contest to the death, with the odds stacked heavily against her. Well, if it was a fight they wanted, it was a fight they would soon get. Strategies began flowing through her head. She began studying her many opponents, their strengths and weaknesses. Then the battle started its course, slowly and cautiously. She scanned the two green men approaching her directly, while the other two separated, spreading out toward the rear. The men in front were grinning to themselves, perhaps believing Jamie to be weak and fragile. In her mind she relished at the idea of proving them wrong, but she had to stay focused on the ones behind as well, no doubt attempting to distract her.

She prepared herself, readying her defensive stance. As the two in front were about to engage, the smaller one stopped the others from advancing.

"*Cocky little fuck*", Jamie thought to herself. She waved at him to bring it, unfazed by her new attire.

"*Come on little man*, I've been itching for a fight." Jamie exclaimed.

The small man was surprisingly fast, bull rushing her with his shoulder, but Jamie avoided the strike, sidestepping to her right. This, as it turned out, was meant to be a distraction. As soon as she evaded the initial attack, she was struck from behind from another's fist that crashed down on her skull. She fell to the ground hard, the pain ringing in her ears. Then the next one struck, kicking her in the ribs before planting her with a furious kick to the face. The force of the impact slammed her body back first to the ground.

"Ughhh!" She shouted as pain now shot up her spine and shoulders. She realized they had no intention of having a fair fight. She was in the gauntlet. Noticing her vulnerable position, the man in red went to stomp on her face, but she rolled out of the way and flipped up to her feet. The move surprised her adversaries. The initial one jumped at her from the right. As he came in close she elbowed him in the temple, dropping him to the ground. She followed that maneuver up by grabbing hold of the next one's head and repeatedly thrusting her knee against his skull. Sensing one to her left, she spun around and punched him squarely in the face.

The Alpha Male came from behind and placed Jamie in a choke hold, slowly suffocating her. While this was happening, another sprinted up close to knee her in the stomach. With instincts, Jamie countered by swinging her legs up in the air and wrapping them around his neck. In this position, still locked in the choke hold, she was able to aggressively drag his entire body to the ground, head first. The red man squeezed her neck even tighter as a result. At that moment, Jamie gained a second wind. She furiously began to drive her elbows into his ribs, over and over again, crashing like razor sharp knives. His grip started to loosen. As it did, she leaned her head forward and then snapped it back with authority, the back of her head crushing against his face. While the effect enabled her to escape the hold, it hurt her as well. She shook her head to regain her composure. This fight was far from over. All five of them were still alive, desperately trying to end her life. Round two was about to commence. Sweat dripped down Jamie's face. Her eyes locked in focus, she took a deep breath and closed her eyes. As she exhaled, she opened her eyes and quickly evaded a strike coming at her from the left. She delivered a roundhouse kick to his face and immediately followed with a side kick to the next man's ribs. Two more engaged simultaneously at an angle. She used her speed, backtracking to match their pace. She then pivoted to the left, taking hold of the man's arm closest to her, locking it in place. With her left arm wrapped around his, she kicked him in the knee cap that bent his body downward. As he was falling, she slid her right arm down to his forearm. She violently bent his arm upward, fracturing the bone in three places. His scream pierced the air. She then wrapped her strong arm around his neck and with full strength, using her other hand as leverage, snapped his neck. One down, four to go. "Take it one step at a time girl, I ain't losing today." She thought to herself.

Unfortunately for her, after the demise of their friend, the others were tossed weapons from the crowd. They were now armed with spears, daggers, and machetes, just another obstacle to overcome. Jamie poised her stance, knowing to survive, she needed to disarm at least one. So it began as it started off, with one deciding to confront her on their own, without backup. The man with the spear inched closer as the three in back merely stood back to watch. The first strike came with a forward thrust toward her stomach. She evaded by leaping backward. From there a strike from above, the blade coming down and diagonal, aiming for her heart. She side stepped to the left to avoid the contact. She tried to time the strikes the best she could. The spear had the length advantage but it was slow, requiring the user to exert more energy with each blow. Again the strike came towards the middle, and again she leaped back. This time, however, as her feet touched the ground, she turned slightly to the left and grabbed hold of the elongated handle with her left hand towards the middle. With her free hand she grabbed the far edge of the handle underneath. Instantaneously, she thrusted her knee upward and ripped through the wood.

She saw before her the perfect opening. She drove the blade directly through the man's stomach as blood gushed from his mouth. She immediately ripped the blade from his stomach and grabbed hold of the back of his head with her left hand. She then rammed the blade through his throat and jaw. His body fell hard against the ground.

The one with the daggers quickly engaged, with more tenacity than the other. He swung at her wildly and furiously. She was blocking each attack with both pieces of the broken spear, keeping pace with her opponent. She couldn't stay like this for long. As she blocked the dagger to the left, she slammed the splintered handle through his foot while blocking the dagger to her right with the bladed piece. That caused the man to drop his weapon and pause. She kicked him in the stomach at a downward angle. The strike dropped him to the ground. She then sprinted towards him and leapt in the air. As she came down she stabbed him with both pieces in his chest. Blood careened against her face. She smiled in rage. Three down, two to go. Maybe now they would back off. She waited for the next to engage. She knew the real contest would come from the red bathed one, the Alpha male. He was studying her movements the entire time, deciphering her strengths and weaknesses.

At that moment she dropped the broken spear to the ground and picked up the fallen daggers. The blades danced and glistened with each strike, reigning down like lightening. During the melee, Jamie adjusted her daggers, blocking inward and up, driving the machetes away from her face. She then rapidly head butted her opponent in the face. He stumbled backward, giving Jamie the opportunity she was looking for. For that slight moment his grip loosened and she brutally chopped off his hands. He screamed in hysteria as blood showered out, staining the ground. Jamie crisscrossed her daggers in front of his throat and ripped through, severing his major arteries. Her face was beginning to look like that of the red man. Suddenly, she let loose a primal roar.

"Raaaaaaaaaaaaaaaaaaaaaah!!" She tossed the daggers aside and lifted up the machetes. Though not her swords, she thought them to be the closest in comparison. The crowd remained silent, as if paralyzed in astonishment. Their warriors were being dwindled down by yet another woman, how humiliating.

The Alpha showed no concern. No woman had ever bested him in combat before and he wasn't about to let this girl stop the trend, especially an American one. True, she was fast, but she had to be fatigued. She had to slip up somewhere, he thought to himself.

Jamie knew he was waiting for her to tire. She twice, slammed her machetes against each other, ringing out a loud echo, calling for him to rise. The Alpha male merely stared at her with hollow eyes, as if staring into her soul. This temporarily dazed Jamie. Before she could even react, he swiftly pulled out a blow dart from his sash and sent it flying, hitting her right leg.

As she tried to step forward, her leg locked in place. She dropped her machetes in an attempt to move her leg with both hands. With her confidence shot to hell, she started to panic, her heart racing, knowing she was completely vulnerable to attack.

The red man sprinted toward her and punched her face repeatedly with both fists. Blood shot from her mouth. She couldn't evade due to the handicap. He then kicked her viciously in the face that slammed her against the ground. Blood and spit spewed out from the impact. The man stomped her face a couple times before picking her up and throwing her across the dirt.

The crowd now erupted in cheers, awoken from their previous state of shock. The Alpha was proving his worth, and soon death would fall upon this brash girl.

Jamie could barely hear them at all, her face bruised all over, and her ribs battered.

"Fuck, was this it?" she thought to herself. "Death by a damn dart, cheap." Bewilderment crossed the Alpha's face as Jamie actually started to laugh out loud. She was laughing, despite faced with a certain demise. The Alpha started to appreciate her fortitude. Unfortunately, that respect was not enough to spare her. She killed four of his own. A debt needed to be paid. He methodically walked toward her, admiring his handiwork. He was amused when she attempted to rise up, only to fall back down again. Jamie desperately tried to conceive a way out, scanning for any possible opening. Once in close proximity, the Alpha bent down and gazed into her eyes. Terror seeped through her veins. With an eerie smile, he punched her in the face, then again, and again, and again. It seemed to never end. She withstood all she could until she abruptly grabbed hold of his face and savagely bit into his eyes as hard as she could, clamping them down like a vice. Using the rest of her might, she pulled them outward and almost tore them from the sockets. His scream sent shockwaves through the crowd. In one final act, she reached into his sash to find anything of use. She felt the tip of a knife and smiled. Salvation at last, she took it out and pierced it through his throat.

"Fuck you." She whispered, completely sapped of strength. Afterward, the young man that trapped her reemerged in front of her. Annoyed once again by his presence, she promptly raised her hand and flipped him off. He smiled, pulling out the sleeping powder. He blew it into her face, sending her to oblivion. Letting his desires get the best of him, he knelt down and gently removed her top. That was not enough for him, however, as he pulled up her bra, revealing those tantalizing nipples. He came close to wrapping his mouth around one but was stopped short by the High King, who was watching the battle. He gave the young man a stern look. The young man retreated back in respect. The High King looked down on the battle hardened warrior, impressed by her ruthlessness and will to survive. She had killed five of his best men single handedly, a feat never once witnessed before. Surely a warrior of this caliber should be recognized for her talents and bravery. Therefore, he put his fingers in the blood pouch and drew an image of a singular flame beneath her right breast. At that moment, the High King signaled for a group of men to carry her to his bedroom. There he would satisfy his hunger.

PART III

Reiyiko kept awake, trying to force out the horrible things she just witnessed. The images of her friend raped and dismembered gave her nightmares, constantly bombarding her head like boulders. She could still smell the foul stench of blood and the taste of vomit that lingered in her throat. Animals, all of them, she said to herself, especially The Scarred Man. The very thought that he was aroused by her spirit repulsed her. She didn't care what accolades he spread upon her. That he thought of her as some kind of spirit animal transcending human form angered her, what hypocrisy. She was simply desperate to survive, what else was she supposed to do? Julia was not below her in any way, she was a human being, a joyful spirit. She was the kind of person Reiyiko looked up to, who she could share all her insecurities with. For someone like that to be ripped apart from this world with such vulgarity boiled her up inside. At that moment she knew just how cruel this world could be. She shuttered to think what The Scarred Man would do next.

Just then she could hear movement coming toward her cell. She felt his presence so strongly. This time he was accompanied by three others with intent. Instead of coming for her, they walked past her cell and headed further down. There she could hear the screams and cries of another captive in the distance. It sounded like Amy Sinclair, the journalist. It was happening all over again.

"No! Get away from me! No! Heeelp!" Amy screamed. When the group unlocked her cage, she attempted to flee, but immediately was hit in the face with sleeping powder. It didn't take long before she fell under it's spell. Reiyiko looked on with fire burning in her veins, watching as the three vermin began stripping her nude. The Scarred Man peered up at Reiyiko and smiled. The time had come to feast again, the dinner bells ringing. He slowly unlocked Reiyiko's cage, hoping she would behave herself.

"It is time to eat my dear, I hope you have learned your lesson." He gestured her to follow him. Reiyiko glared at him but said nothing. She followed him in protest, watching as Amy's unconscious body was being carried to the dinner table. The roars of the crowd waiting in anticipation hardened her heart. They gently laid Amy down and restrained her wrists and ankles. A couple got their licks in, sampling her nipples before The Chef emerged once more. This time he brought a young apprentice with him, who happened to be the same young man she encountered before. Revulsion swept across Reiyiko's face but she remained stoic. The apprentice was eager to get started, his tongue licking his lips. When The Chef was unwrapping the tools for the job, the apprentice rushed to grab the large carving knife. The Chef stopped him from following through. He wanted to teach him the art of tasting the meal first. The apprentice understood his meaning, now more insatiable than before. He climbed on the table and sat upon her waist. Wasting little time, he slithered his tongue across every section of her delicious stomach, moving slowly. When his tongue reached her navel it stopped there and began swirling against every crevasse like a snake. Once finished licking, he dove his nose inside and breathed in all the sweet aromas. The Chef grinned at the sight, loving everything he saw. The apprentice continued to attack her navel, pressing his lips inside repeatedly, his saliva soiling every inch of it. Taking his cue, The Chef proceeded to lick down her leg, until opening his mouth and sucking her toes. It was like a sensual orgy had erupted. Once finished with her navel, he licked in between her breasts before placing his mouth around one of her nipples. He sucked on it long and hard as his left hand groped away at her other breast. Done with her nipples he kissed her lips while brushing back her luscious blonde hair. He then licked her cheeks and the bridge of her nose.

This violation seemed to last a lifetime until it finally stopped. Now the time had come for the consumption of the flesh. The Chef guided the apprentice to the knife and helped him carve. Much the same as Julia, the blade pierced below Amy's breast and was pulled down to her navel. The apprentice then pulled out her heart and bit down. He shared it with the Chef as well. Blood trickled down her abdomen and onto the table. The bell sounded and then, like savage creatures of the night, the rest of the group didn't bother with manners, ripping and tearing away at her flesh with their teeth. Others brought machetes with them and cut off parts of her limbs, fighting each other like wild dogs for a piece of the meat.

Reiyiko looked on unfazed, as if desensitized to the madness. The situation grew dire with each waiting minute, with no end left in sight.

Rachel was sitting in the corner of her cell when she heard the rustling of footsteps in the distance. Closer and closer it came. As they came into view, her eyes widened with surprise and enthusiasm, which was strange, it wasn't a promising sight.

"*Jamie!*" She yelled out. It was Jamie O'Neil, Ray's partner and best friend. She wasn't looking particularly good at the moment. She was half nude and unconscious, being carried by a group of men led by the High King himself. His presence was intimidating enough. Blood had stained her mouth and several bruises were scattered about her face. Her ribs appeared battered as well. Rachel noticed that Jamie had a marking just below her breasts, a singular flame. Dread filled her soul to see Jamie treated like this. She awoke Bruce from his slumber.

"Bruce, Bruce, look, it's Jamie, they must be here." Bruce groggily came to.

"Shit, what the hell happened to her? Looks like she's been in a war."

"I don't know, but we have to do something."

"What can we do? We have to be vigilant and stand by at the moment. Besides, Jamie is tough, she can take care of herself." The thought did not ease Rachel's heart in the slightest. Rachel and Bruce simply watched as Jamie was brought further down the tunnel. As they approached the High King's quarters, two men stood guard at his door. When they saw him they promptly opened the wooden door for him.

At first, Jamie was placed on the brown fur rug that lay to the left of The High King's bed. There, the men who carried her began removing the rest of her garments until she was completely bare. They took wet soaked rags and began cleaning her wounds, preparing her for the ceremony later that night. Once clean, they hoisted her up and placed her gently on the bed. She looked so peaceful and beautiful to the High King, who then ordered his men to leave. Though he wished her no harm, he still could not allow her to escape. He lifted her arms up behind her head and secured them to the bed with a silk cloth. He then straightened out her legs and tied her ankles to the edge of the bed with another cloth. The High King slowly smelled the entirety of her body before brushing her hair back. A clay jar of fresh honey was on the small table to his right. He took the jar and began pouring a streak of honey from her waistline all the way down between her breasts. Not satisfied quite yet, the High King poured more into her navel, filling the gaping hole. The pleasure should not belong only to him he thought. It was time to awaken the young warrior.

He dipped his finger in the smelling salts, placing it under her nose. Jamie woke up to the sweet aroma of honey. She looked down and saw the High King on top of her, reveling in the masterpiece he created. Her eyes widened with shock before turning to embarrassment when she saw his tongue creep out of his mouth. When he saw her blush with potency, he grinned and sat his tongue on her belly. From there he slithered it up to her navel. She moaned out in ecstasy, then bit down on her lower lip as his tongue submerged in the pool of honey in her navel. He swirled it around every crevasse, her eyes rolling up toward her head in response. The feeling was utterly intoxicating. He continued his playfulness, sliding his tongue between her breasts. More moans emerged from her mouth as he began sucking upon her nipples one at a time. The warrior that she was, was replaced by a vulnerable woman, shackled by depravity. The High King saw something special within her, he was completely infatuated. Finished with her voluptuous breasts, he opened her mouth with his fingers and dipped his tongue down her throat. The kiss felt like a roller coaster of euphoria, she couldn't help herself. It was almost as if she became a slave to his every whim. He owned her mind, body, and soul at that moment. Jamie was alone and trapped, unable to fight back. Fully satisfied, The High King released his tongue from her mouth and whispered strange words she could not understand. In his final act of pleasure, he kissed the tip of her nose and pricked her neck with a concoction of tranquilizer, sending her to a blissful sleep once more.

PART IV

The team headed deeper through the jungle in search of Jamie. Jackson and McPherson led the way in front, while Rivers and Wu Long were flanked on either side. In the back rear was McBride. They moved swiftly and silently like the wind, tracking any movements or sounds around them. Moving closer, Jackson could hear faint noises in front of them. He signaled the team and they slowed to a crawl. Using the thick trees as cover, they inched closer, witnessing a group of eight to ten men conversing amongst themselves, unaware of the danger that was hunting them. It seemed too easy, gathering in an open area of the wood. Yet, as if sensing their presence at the last second, the men disbanded in several directions, seemingly blending into the environment. This put the team on high alert, walking slowly past the open area until entering the vast jungle once more. The hissing of snakes and the callings of birds and insects provided constant distractions, giving advantage to their adversaries lurking about. This was their territory and they knew how to disappear within its trenches.

"Spread out, they know we're coming." Whispered Jackson. They opened their ears to the sounds below and above, trying to pinpoint their opponents' locations. Thunder began to emanate throughout the island. A storm was brewing. Just then, Jackson could hear the slight movement of leaves crinkling in the background behind him. His instincts kicked in as he saw within his peripheral, a figure jump down a tree with intent to ambush him from behind. Jackson countered the attack by grabbing the man by his shoulders and throwing him with great velocity against a tree. The man's back was torn from the impact. Without thought, Jackson rushed at the man and delivered a bone rattling knee to his face, ripping away bark from the tree. He kneed him again in the face before lifting him up and driving the back of his skull against the tree, again and again. He smashed the man's face in with his boot. Sensing others further ahead, Jackson moved from tree to tree, slowly and methodically, trying to block his enemies' line of sight.

As Mai was walking in between the trees, one emerged from the shadows as if he was a trained ninja. Instantaneously, she forced out her Sai's and slid toward him on her knees, slashing his ankles. This caused his weapons to drop to the ground. Mai then thrusted upward and stabbed him in the lungs. As she retracted them he gasped for air, but none would come. From there she viciously stabbed him in both ear drums, squirting out blood. She couldn't rest for long, however, as another came from behind and elbowed her in the back of the head. She fell down to her knees and dropped her Sai's. The man tried to bend her neck back and slit her throat, but she rolled forward to dodge the attack. The pace sped up. She dodged numerous strikes from her opponent before finding her stride with a blistering sweep kick that derailed his progress. In a remarkable move, she somersaulted in the air and kicked him in the temple. She slid forward and grabbed her Sai's in fluent motion. She then spun around as he was getting up and threw her Sai's in his eyes. With anger embedded in her face, she ripped them from his eyes and continued the hunt.

Sam was next on their radar. His Beretta's were poised and ready. His eyes were keen like a hawk's as he saw two adversaries hiding in the trees a few feet away. He put two bullets in one and three in the other. He put two bullets in the chest of the next man before the first had fallen to the ground. When the next fell, he put another bullet between his eyes to be certain. Even more came out of their hiding places. Sam spun around and delivered two bullets in the next one's face and three to the one next to him, all center mass. These men were skilled, but not quite skilled enough to deal with this formidable enemy, each with the determination of a pack of lions.

Laura put her skills as a sniper to good use. She knew she was at her deadliest from above. If her challengers used the trees as an advantage, she would use them as well. She ascended up a thick tree to her liking, moving like a gymnast up the branches until she found the perfect one. She crawled slowly on the sturdy branch, using the strength of her legs to maintain a solid grip. She carefully removed her weapon that lay across her back and peered through the scope. Scanning the area slowly, she captured one to her far right. She zoomed in on the man's head, waited patiently, and pulled the trigger. He dropped like a fish, his body remaining on the branch. One down, she said to herself. Laura saw another lurking further ahead, his hand grasping on a machete, looking for a surprise ambush. Instead, she smiled and locked on to his face. The next impact teared through the bridge of his nose and out the back of his head. Just then rain began to pour from the skies above.

Ray found himself surrounded by five enemies. He removed his favorite weapon, the mighty sledgehammer. He looked on, unfazed by his predicament. He struck immediately, slamming the hammer hard on the first one's head, splitting his skull open. He countered the next man to his left with a crushing blow to his ribcage, causing him to stumble to the ground. Abruptly, he spun around on one knee and delivered a strike to the next one's ankle, shattering the bone in two. He followed it up with a savage hit across his face, breaking his nose and ripping out an eye in the process. Refocused on his next attacker, he blocked the machete with the metallic handle of his sledgehammer. He then kicked him in the groin, sending him to his knees. This was followed by a brutal strike to his jugular. Ray's face became bathed in the blood of his adversaries. Still two remained, including the man with the shattered ribcage. He would finish him off last. First he dealt with the fresh one, armed with a bow and arrow. The man pulled back the string and let one loose. Ray deflected the arrow with the sledgehammer and rammed the hammer diagonally down on his face. He raised the sledgehammer high above his head and sent it crashing down on the man's face again, pulverizing it to shreds. This left the last victim, who was still clutching his chest in pain. Ray paced toward him with a piercing glare. The man's face cringed in fear as he started crawling backward.

"*No.*" Ray said as he methodically came in closer. Ray stepped down on his already broken ribs, allowing him to suffer in agony. He then raised his hammer up and drove it with great force on his neck, snapping it. Afterward, as Ray continued the search for his partner, he stumbled upon a ravine. Across the ravine he noticed a large structure resembling a fortress. Perhaps here was where Jamie was. Ray waited momentarily before approaching. He called out over his radio for re-enforcements.

"Bone-Crusher, come in, over." No response.

"Hey, Riker." whispered Mai, who was tracking him closely after her battle.

"How many did you get?"

"Two."

"Got you beat, put down five of those bastards." Suddenly, Bone-Crusher replied over his radio.

"Riker, I'm here with Raven and Winchester. What's your status?, over."

"Got Shell Shock with me, I've come across a fortress of some kind. It's got be where Jamie and the others are."

"Great, what's your location, we'll head to you soon." Replied Bone-Crusher.

"It's located south, just across a small ravine. We'll hold our positions till you get here."

"Sounds good, over."

PART V

The High King was preparing Jamie for the Ceremony of the Enlightened Warrior, a rite of passage to those surpassing the rank of Alpha. This particular ceremony held the distinction of being the most unprecedented. For the first time since the formation of the Cannibal Horde, a female attained such an honor. Jamie O'Neil had bested five men, including the once undefeated Alpha. This was her night of recognition. She was to be first bathed in the waters of purity, layered with coconut butter and honey. Next, her body would be submerged in the blood of her fallen opponents, symbolizing the heart of brutality. From there she would be affixed with the robe of the high Alpha, cut at the midriff and adorned with layers of gem stones and crystalized leaves. A crown of skull and bone would be placed upon her head. It was not an honor that Jamie looked forward to in the slightest. Pride in the warrior spirit was one thing, but cannibalizing the weak was something different entirely. The celebration was a few hours away. Jamie held on to hope that her friends would provide the fireworks. The Scarred Man of course, would be attending the affair accompanied by his most prized possession. Reiyiko could not stand the sight of him, especially those perverted eyes that were always watching. She kept looking for a means to escape in the meantime.

Avery Jackson led Laura and Sam down the path as indicated by Riker. About half way toward their destination, Jackson's sixth sense kicked in. He realized they were being followed. It seemed more adversaries lurked in the ensuing darkness.

"Get ready, we got more coming." Jackson relayed to his team. Before long, however, they could see more enemies coming from every direction, quickly swarming them like angry hornets. They were about to be in the thick of things. Though the fight would soon be futile, there was no fear displayed. The group converged on Avery, who responded by grabbing two by the neck and tossing them toward the wall of humanity. He then kicked another in the ribs before aggressively breaking his neck. Sam followed suit, taking down multiple hostiles before he was eventually disarmed by the massive group. Laura was next, whipping out her double edged knives, carving and tearing through several opponents. The melee was finally put to rest when three sets of bags containing sleeping powder were thrown in the center of the pile. The effect knocked the three of them out, while taking down a number of the group in the process. No matter, they had succeeded in capturing their tormentors. It was now their turn to inflict the torment, starting with the purple haired girl.

"I don't like this, they should have been here by now." said Riker.
"What do you wanna do?" Asked Mai.
"We can't worry about that for now, we have to go in."
"Agreed." Riker and Mai creeped toward the structure, staying low. When they got in range of the back entrance, they witnessed two guards on either side, armed with spears. Ray motioned to Mai, who removed her Sai's. They moved silently, backs to the walls. As soon as Mai saw an opportunity, she came up behind them both and slit their throats. Mai and Riker immediately dragged the bodies off undetected. The cool night was approaching as the rain started to subside. At that moment, they moved like shadows in the devil's den. More guards stood within a few feet of them down the hall way. They hid in the empty crevasses. Instead of wasting their energy, they waited for them to pass out of sight. Afterward, they advanced, searching for any signs of Rachel or Jamie. Just then they could hear noises to the right of their location. Moving swiftly, as they came across the cell doors they were intercepted by four

guards. There was no use for subtlety any longer. Riker forced out his knife and slashed one across the stomach before driving it through his neck. Reiyiko looked on from her cell and was grateful to see a familiar face. Mai slashed the man against his wrists and thrust the Sai's through his throat. She retracted and engaged the next coming at her from the left. She savagely kicked him in the knee cap before spinning around the back of him. There she slit his throat with both Sai's. Blood whipped sporadically on the walls. Riker had disposed of the last one standing guard, sending a knife through his right eye. Mai rushed to Reiyiko with enthusiasm, her best friend was still alive.

"Reiyiko! Thank God." She said as she smiled.

Reiyiko returned the smile as relief finally fell upon her face.

"Mai Wu Long, it's great to see your face." She glanced up at Riker as well.

"Ray, I don't know where they have taken Rachel and Bruce. This man with scars upon his face has kept me isolated, treating me like some sort of mythical goddess, guy gives me the creeps."

"What about Jamie? Did you see Jamie?" Riker asked.

"No, sorry, I hope you brought more allies."

"Yeah, but we lost contact with them a while ago."

The news concerned Reiyiko.

"That's not good." Riker looked at her a bit puzzled from what she was wearing.

Reiyiko noticed as well.

"I know what you're thinking. The scarred man made me put this on, for some kind of ceremony tonight."

Suddenly, they could hear movement coming down the far side of the hall and the ringing of bells.

"That must be the scarred man now, the ceremony must be happening."

"Ok, let him take you there, we will shadow you." She nodded at him in approval.

—ᴍ—

Somewhere deep in the underground tunnels, Laura spit out blood as she was hit in her exposed stomach with a large rock. She grunted again as the rock struck once more, forming welts upon her body. She was tied to the ceiling with vines. Another strike came against the side of her ribs, causing more blood to spew from her mouth. They didn't bother placing her in the death pit. She had already killed four of their kind and displayed a cockiness behind it.

Elsewhere, Avery was being tortured as well. Restrained to the wall he was repeatedly struck in the face with edged rocks. This only infuriated the large man. It would take more than mere rocks to cripple his vigor. Sam was last to be seen, being whipped with shredded rope against his back. It tore pieces of skin away as he was grinding his teeth in pain. While this was occurring the other members of the cult were gathering together at the ceremonial meeting place. A centerpiece of sticks and branches were being ignited by the ritual fires. The flames rose majestically in the air. Large stones were encircled around the centerpiece, providing room for the dancers and musicians emerging from the woods. The sounds of their music could be heard throughout the fortress. The Scarred Man arrived at Reiyiko's cell to escort her to the festivities. Riker and Mai followed them unseen. The gathering increased in size as the drums grew louder. The dancers were half nude, adorned with markings upon their bodies. They swayed and swooned to the music, moving as if one with the melodies. They exuded a somewhat supernatural appearance. Soon the High King and the warrior of honor would be joining them at the high seats that sat in the rear of the circle. Jamie looked like that of a queen, her exposed skin only made her appear more powerful and mystical. Red and green leaves were being tossed on the ground as she walked with the High King to their seats. They faced the crowd. The High King then produced from his sash a neckless made of slices of heart from the previous victims.

As the ceremony was in progress, Avery worked at the roots that were restricting his arms. Using his strength, he ripped and tore away at them, gradually weakening their hold. A lone adversary in charge of standing guard heard the tussling and started to engage the prisoner.

Avery feigned complacency, before he ripped through his restraints. He grabbed the man with both hands while compressing his head and pushing his thumbs into his eyes. He pushed his eyes in until they reached the man's brain. He then hoisted him up in the air and plunged his back straight down on his knee, breaking it in half. A smile ran across Avery's face as he saw his weapons in the corner. With the rest of the cult focused on the ceremony outside, he used the opportunity to spring the others. As Avery carefully approached Laura's cell, he observed two guards outside her door, laughing at her injuries. The kill would come easy for Bone-Crusher. As the guards taunted Laura, Avery came directly behind them, waiting. Before they could react to his presence, he pulled out two knives and aggressively slit their throats. Afterward, he kicked down the door and cut Laura from her restraints.

"Raven, *Raven!* look at me, you Ok? *Talk to me girl.*" Laura's speech was weak, but she still had strength left within her spirit. She tried to mask the pain as best she could.

"...Yeah, yeah, I'm ready to go." But before she could step forward, she began to lose her balance. Avery caught her as she was falling down.

"Shit, you're in no condition to fight. Judging by your wounds, I'm afraid you might have internal bleeding."

Laura refused to admit it.

"*Bullshit*, I'll be fine, you still got that shot of adrenaline right?" The question concerned Avery.

"Yeah, but it won't last long, it's too dangerous, given your state." She grabbed him firmly by the arm with little strength she had left, urging him to reconsider.

"Just do it, *do it!* I'm not sitting on the sidelines."

Avery gave her a look of caution. He then removed the syringe, pausing a moment.

"*Fuck it.*" He then injected it in her arm. She felt the effect immediately, her heart racing like a hurricane. She re-armed herself with a renewed sense of enthusiasm. Next thing was releasing Sam. Before they could get to him, however, he had already dispatched of the guards, kicking one through the door. Avery smiled when he saw him.

"Haven't lost your touch I see." Avery said.

"Nah, it was easy" Sam replied.

"Let's hunt some cannibals." Avery said with intensity. Meanwhile, the ceremony was about to reach its fever pitch. It could not be complete without the ritual feast. The horns blasted forth and out came the main course, Rachel McTavern. She was struggling against her restraints as they were bringing her out on the serving table. She screamed out in protest.

"No! Let me go!" When Jaime saw her, her instinct was to attack, but she would be easily outnumbered. She could only watch, hoping for a solution. Bruce was present as well, being dragged by the rope that tied his wrists together. He was there to watch as his lover was to be sacrificed, fed to her own friend, Jamie O'Neil.

"Bastards!" Bruce yelled out to the crowd. Ray and Mai were lying in wait, but were soon rejoined by the rest of the team.

"Ray, Mai." Avery whispered.

"Heh, I'm glad to see you all in one piece, though Laura seems a little worse for wear."

"She'll be good for a bit, had to shoot her up with adrenaline to keep her head on straight."

"Never knew how to stop fighting. Payback is a bitch." Laura said.

"You bet your *ass.*" Replied Sam. As Rachel continued to struggle, one of the men blew the sleeping smoke into her face. She fell to its effect in an instant. At that moment, The High King grinned as The Chef came out, seemingly to begin the ritualistic carving. However, as soon as he approached, The High King stopped him. Curiosity filled his mind at the sudden halt. Instead, the High King unwrapped the cloth and motioned for Jamie to come forward.

As she did, The High King presented her with the carving knife. She looked at him in protest and astonishment, that he actually thought she would murder her friend, what absurdity. Yet, The High King again, urged her to partake in the gruesome act. She needed to think fast. She paused and took a good moment to scan the people in attendance. Then she saw the team lying in wait, blending in with the cult. She noticed

Mai closing in on the perimeter, moving toward Bruce McTavern. Bruce looked on, worrying about Rachel's fate, praying for a miracle. He knew in the back of his mind, however, that Jamie had to intention of following through with it. He looked at her intently. Jamie looked directly in his eyes as she took hold of the knife. Just then she winked her eye at him. All hell was about to break loose. Jamie turned around in front of The High King and struck. The blade ran up his throat and out through the top of his skull. Shock was etched across his dead face as the cult erupted in fury.

Instantaneously, Jamie slashed The Chef against his throat and leaped up toward Bruce's direction. She aimed the blade perfectly, slicing through the rope restraining his wrists. Mai reacted as well, handing Bruce a pair of double edged knives. From the commotion, Reiyiko kicked The Scarred Man in the ribs that leveled him to the ground. As she heard the two grenades fall in the center of the crowd, she dove forward and tackled Jamie, who was being pulled back by members of the cult. At the same time, Bruce freed Rachel and carried her toward safety, placing her down out of sight. Three seconds later, the explosion rocked the group, tearing apart limbs and ripping out organs. Bloody carnage was strewn everywhere as most of the people were panicking. This was the moment the team was looking for and they didn't waste the opportunity. Bruce took out several with his knives, severing arms and shredding intestine. Ray forced out his shotgun, putting a bullet through a man's mouth that exploded out portions of his brain. He then shot another that tore through his chest. Mai worked with her Sai's, piercing eyes and throats swiftly and effectively. Five lunged on top of Avery, doing their best to bring him down.

Avery bent down and pulled away at his enemies, sending them flying through the air like javelins, hitting hard against the ground. He put on his brass knucks and started hammering away, reigning down brutality with all his fury. Sam and Laura followed suit, sending bullets through heads. During the ensuing melee, The Scarred Man had eluded the strike force, crawling away from the scene. As he saw Rachel in his cross hairs, he quietly inched toward her. He hoped the distraction paid off for him as well. After Reiyiko dispatched two more, she quickly started looking for the Scarred Man. It was then when she noticed Riker and Bruce, and followed in their direction. As the battle appeared nearing its conclusion, Riker and Bruce noticed what the Scarred Man was doing and followed him. Sensing their presence as well, the Scarred Man sprung up and sprinted toward Rachel. He picked her up and scurried like a rat. Upon seeing this, they engaged in the pursuit, leaving the rest of the team to fend for themselves. Mai forced her Sai through the last one's throat and smiled as the team stood in victory.

"*Hells yeah!*" Exclaimed Jamie.

"Great to see you alive and kicking Blade. I believe these belong to you." said Avery as he handed Jamie her Katana blades. She smiled at him.

"Yeah, you know, a girl can only take the abuse for so long." Out of nowhere, however, the moment passed as a large brute of a man appeared in front of them. He had four scars down his chest with eyes that were almost pure white. He stood at six feet two and every inch of him was bathed in red. His arms were like tree trunks and he held two enormous axes. The team prepared themselves for the final boss, slowly surrounding him. They realized they needed everything in their arsenal to survive this abomination. Sam and Laura opted to start first, raising their firearms in hopes of a quick fight. However, when they pulled the triggers nothing came out. The bullets had already been spent much to their chagrin. That initial confidence was replaced by worried eyes.

The brute plunged his axes straight at them. Sam and Laura rolled out of the way. Jamie slashed him twice in the ankle. The attack barely did anything at all. Instead she was leveled with a furious kick to the face, knocking her out in the process. The unfortunate turn of events was not lost on the rest of the team, but they needed to push on.

While Avery engaged the behemoth, Mai and the others got around his back side. Avery hammered away at his abdomen with the brass knuckles, trying to inflict the maximum amount of damage. As this was happening, Mai leaped up in the air and plunged her Sai's into his back, but she was quickly shrugged off. With a large machete she acquired from a fallen enemy, Laura severed the big man's hand. He bellowed out in rage before ramming his elbow directly in her face, blood pouring from his open wound. The force rattled her cranium as she fell hard to the ground. The adrenaline, however, allowed her to bounce back up and continue the attack with furious kicks to his ribs. The brute swung wildly at Sam's head with the remaining axe. He sidestepped out of the way and delivered a vicious kick to his knee cap, dropping him to one knee. Seeing him slumped over, Avery stepped on the axe and ripped it from the man's hand. He then swung it horizontally against his chest, splashing out droplets of blood. The big man seemed to be made of solid stone. He grabbed Laura's throat and squeezed with all his might.

Laura's eyes began to bulge as the panic set in, her hands flailing about. Avery punched him squarely in the face with the brass knuckles. That shot broke the man's nose. He head-butted Avery, dazing him while he maintained his grip on Laura's throat, squeezing even harder. She started to fall into death's grip as her face turned purple. Mai burst into action and thrust her Sai's through his ribs, then violently tore into his upper chest cavity near his heart. Still, it was not enough to keep him down, his will to live was extraordinary. Just as it seemed Laura would let out her final breath, out of nowhere, a resurgent Jamie O'Neil sprinted toward him. She severed his arm with one sword while the other slit his throat. Laura barely clung to life, finally finding relief. Jamie, not satisfied, aggressively cut off his head for certainty. She then felt the need to spit upon his face.

"*Mother fucker.* That was nuts. You Ok Laura?"

Laura was coughing from the assault, a large red mark visible on her throat.

"...Yeah" She coughed again. "I owe you one, thought I was a goner at first."

"Nah, I got your back, sorry for the delayed reaction, that guy was a freak."

"*Woah! What a rush!!*" Exclaimed Avery. "You guys all right?"

"Yes sir boss, we be *bringing the fire!*" Said Sam.

Elsewhere, Rachel was starting to come to from the sleeping gas.

When she soon realized she was being carried by The Scarred Man, she shouted out wildly. The Scarred Man snapped back at her.

"*Be quiet woman!*" In that moment, however, he noticed a presence gaining speed behind him.

"*Put her down! Now!*" Yelled Bruce. When The Scarred Man turned around, he had a knife positioned on Rachel's throat. Abruptly, Riker came up next to Bruce, now with a shotgun aimed at The Scarred Man's face.

"*Stay back!*" yelled The Scarred Man. "Stay back or I'll kill her." For the first time, fear crossed his mind as sweat began to trickle down his face.

"*Shoot him Ray! Shoot him now!*" Cried out Rachel, begging him to pull the trigger.

"*Shut up! Put the gun down!* I'll kill her, *I'll slit her fucking throat!*" Riker slightly hesitated, his mind racing for a way to end this without hurting Rachel. The Scarred Man yelled out again.

"*Put it down, now! I'm not fucking around!*" At that moment Riker slowly started to lower his weapon, despite every urge to put a bullet through his brain. Rachel desperately wanted him to reconsider, her face riddled in protest. Bruce, however, had other ideas in mind.

"*No!* Put it down Riker, I'm begging you."

"What are you doing Bruce?" Asked Rachel.

"I'm protecting you, you're not gonna die on my watch." Bruce looked at Riker.

"Riker, just do what he says, please."

Riker placed his weapon on the ground.

"Thanks." said The Scarred Man. As soon as he did however, he pulled out a gun that lay hidden behind his belt. He pulled the trigger. It seemed like everything was happening in slow motion. Riker turned his head at Bruce, his eyes lost in horror. The bullet found its way through Bruce's head, ripping out blood and brain matter from his skull.

Rachel fell to disbelief, before elbowing The Scarred Man in the ribs while the knife lowered away from her throat. With fury erupting in his veins, Riker immediately rolled forward and grabbed hold of the shotgun. Before he could pull the trigger, Ray was struck in the back of the head with a rock, knocking him unconscious. Rachel screamed out in shock but was met with a blow dart to the neck. Darkness ensued.

The demon that lay dormant within his soul began to awake. A flash bombarded his eyes, and then another. Again and again it came. Then he saw it looking back at him, breathing heavily, spewing out smoke from its mouth. It was looking directly into his soul, feeding it with hate, with rage. A storm was festering within his heart as flames scorched his eyes and scolded his chest. It grew, stronger and stronger, burning with potency. Once the devil takes hold, beware the wrath of vengeance, for it has no bounds. Mercy is lost in the sea of fire.

In the distance a boat could be seen drifting away from the island. Three figures were present aboard. One was The Scarred Man. The others were the young apprentice and Reiyiko Lee Chang. Suddenly, The Scarred Man spoke.

"Good my dear. You have come back to me."

"I now see it clearly, I have transcended. I am forever yours."

"Excellent. Now the reckoning shall come. The world will know the name Desmond Reaper.

CHAPTER 4
Eve of the Damned

Lisa was getting ready for the symphony, her nerves still shot from the pain. Sweat protruded down her face and the mere thought of stroking the strings gave her chills. Regardless of this sensation she still agreed to this. Was it out of desperation to dull the pain or an effort to prove her resiliency under the circumstances, no matter how bleak? In either case she was going to perform while concealing her true feelings. Did she see her mother in the background or her father's eyes when he looked at her at the funeral? Those hollow eyes, reeked with despair. Suddenly, she heard a knock on the door.

"Lisa, we have to go now." Lynn said as Lisa opened the door.

"Ok, I'm just about ready."

"How do I look?" Lisa asked.

"Epic as usual, you're going to kick ass on that solo."

"Indeed, I am the best cellist of them all." Lisa responded sarcastically.

"Well, only second to moi." They laughed and proceeded to the show. It was a way to settle the tension between them, but it was all a lie.

6:50P.M.

I was getting ready for my daughter's symphony. I had a nice suit for the occasion that would cover over up the "other" one. Upstairs, I put my sledgehammer, knives, smoke grenades, lighter fluid, grappling hook, and skull mask in the black duffle bag. With the tools packed I went to the mirror to fix my tie. Suddenly, a flash of red swarmed my eyes, then it disappeared. I took nothing of it and continued to prepare. It was just about time for me to leave. It was the symphony before the inevitable devastation.

7:55P.M.

Lisa could hear the sound of the crowd, waiting in anticipation. She sat alone in the corner of the stage. She interlocked her hands and pressed them against her forehead. She whispered a prayer for her mother, and a silent one for her father. The time approached, the curtain raised, and the show was about to begin. She had center stage as she scanned the many people in attendance. Her cello was poised and ready to mystify the audience. It had begun. Her hands perfectly blended with the movements of her arms. It was a vision to relish. Her eyes closed to the beauty of the sound emanating from her instrument.

A couple of minutes into the piece I entered the auditorium. I saw my daughter effortlessly stroke the strings, completely focused on the task before her. She was a master at work. I stood in awe as the mesmerizing sound engulfed the auditorium. A proud feeling swept through my otherwise poisoned heart. At the same time the menacing beast started to claw its way out, violently looking for the opening to my soul. I immersed myself with the riveting music before me until the time was right. In the middle of the symphony my mind began to play tricks on me. I saw flashes left and right, repeatedly blinking in my eyes. I saw images of blood and fire, followed by the image of my wife on a cross, screaming out my name. The fire was burning her alive and blood poured from her body.

Suddenly, I saw my daughter open her eyes and scream *"Vengeeeeaaaance!!!"* At that moment my eyes opened back to reality. I could hear him, pounding in my head, it was relentless. The utter determination of the beast was unfathomable.

11:00P.M.

How time flies. Already the assault was lingering, ready to ignite. With the show at its climax I went to my jeep with vengeance tearing through my veins. My destination was forty-five minutes away. I began to unbutton my shirt, revealing the black bullet proof vest. My eyes blared with unbridled and dangerous ecstasy. The plan was about to commence.

PART II: The Devil's Grip

11:59P.M.

The hour was approaching. I put on my gloves and skull mask while waiting in anticipation for the attack. In the background I could hear them all, laughing and rejoicing like a group of proud champions. The smell of filets permeated the atmosphere. Outside, I noticed Wallace had doubled the foot patrol around the structure. He did his due diligence in an attempt to thwart me. What he failed to account for was my cutthroat desire to kill, regardless of consequence.

12:00A.M.

I hid amongst the bushes surrounding the mansion. In my view I could see six armed guards, all covering the entrance. I remained crouched, peering through the skull mask. From the duffle bag I took out three smoke grenades. Holding them in my hand I slowly flipped off all the pins. Without thought, I threw them towards the unexpected guards. Three sets of fumes ignited from the cylinders, blinding their line of sight. It provided the necessary opening.

I moved smoothly through the air and smoke, stalking my prey. When I came in close I already had my knives poised for the strike. I lunged forward at the first two and watched as my blades crisscrossed in front of their throats. It happened so fast. The blades reached their intended targets. Blood flowed from their necks. With instincts and a fluid motion, I reversed the blades and thrust them into the chests of the two guards behind me. My eyes never looked at them but remained locked on the final two in front of me. In an instant, I re-positioned my knives and rolled forward. As I did I slashed them across their stomachs. They were still alive, so I raised my knives and viciously thrust them down into their necks. Their blood leaped upward and caught my mask.

At that moment I grabbed the grappling hook. I swiftly propelled up to the top with my bag around my shoulder. As I reached the top I could see the glass window in the center of the roof. I peered through the glass to see the people below and the six additional vermin with them. Pretty stiff party to have armed thugs invited. Hopefully my presence would lighten the mood. The time had come to take her out. Arming myself with the sledgehammer and with overwhelming malice I did just that. Finding a crease, I immediately launched myself through the glass and rolled forward after reaching the bottom of the ballroom. All the guests screamed in terror when they saw the deranged man holding a sledgehammer. Horrified, they all scattered out of the room to escape.

This left the remaining henchmen all alone. Slowly, I raised my head and gazed at my enemies, all seemingly shocked at what just transpired. I grasped the hammer tight and steady. By the time they could react I was already set in motion. I took the hammer and thrust it into the gut of the first one I saw. He spit out blood from his mouth as he grabbed his stomach in pain. At the same time, with full strength I swung it around my head and connected with the next one's hand, causing his weapon to drop to the floor. I followed it up with a direct shot to his jugular. Re-focused on the initial one, I pivoted to my right and swung the hammer to crush his skull. Blood exploded against my mask. Without even thinking I threw the sledge up in the air, caught it and rammed it with full force against the new comer's face. The force rattled his brain. To my left, I could see the next one coming at me with a knife. I dodged the attack and swung the hammer against his knee cap. He screamed in agony and fell to the floor. I finished him off by ramming the hammer straight down on his neck, easily breaking it. This left the last one too terrified to aim his machine gun.

Instantaneously, I bent down, aimed the hammer vertically, and threw it with great force against his chest.

Wallace had the audacity to appear then. He took a shot at me and missed.

I took out my sidearm and blew off his fucking hand. He screamed like a whore. I casually retrieved my sledgehammer, already soaked in blood. As I turned and looked at him his fear was overwhelming. I pressed the hammer against his throat when the begging started.

"Please.......don't......I beg you, I'll give....you......anything." I pressed it harder down on his throat, slowly suffocating him.

".........What...do you...want?...."

"Reaper, where is he?"

"What? I....don't......know......what you're......talking about." In defiance, I took off my mask. He looked on in absolute horror.

"You're going to tell me his location, or I'm gonna *break your larynx....Where is he?!!"*

".........fuck you."

"Now, is not the time to *fuck* with me."I continued to put pressure on his neck. *Where is he?! Mother fucker!! I will not hesitate."*

".......hahaha, He's coming........for her. Too busy......dealing.... with me. Lisa....will.........die...heh."

"That......was a *mistake.*

, Ahhhhhhhhhhhhhhhh" With that ferocious scream I lifted up the hammer and violently slammed it on his face. His blood doused my face. I stayed there, stoic and still, taking in the moment. This mission was not yet complete, however. I removed the lighter fluid from the bag and proceeded to pour it on the entire floor. Exiting the room I lit a match and tossed it on the floor. The flames were beautiful. I walked down the stairs as the fire continued to burn the mansion. Time, however, was not on my side. Reaper was going after my daughter and I had to stop him before he did. How could I have been so stupid? First thing is first, I needed my pissed off partner for the job. She did have her uses after all.

3:00 A.M.

She woke up to the sound of chains rattling. She could smell a mixture of steel and stale blood in the room. Lynn's first reaction was fear. She was, however, more concerned with the whereabouts of Lisa. When her eyes refocused, she noticed she had been completely stripped and shackled to a metal table. Frantically, she looked right and left for her friend but she was nowhere to be seen.

"Lisa!! Lisa!!, Can you hear me?!" she screamed into the air. She began to shiver as her skin moved on the cold surface. From the corner of her eye she saw her clothes in the corner. As she turned her head a hand embraced her throat. Reaper peered directly into her eyes, eyes soaked with fear. Her heart rate jumped to overdrive. She tried to scream for help but her mouth remained frozen. His other hand caressed her abdomen. A slight tilt of his head, he began to take in the sweet aroma.

"Shhhh, It's alright, soon it'll be over for you. As for your friend, you need not worry; I'm saving her for last. Right now, she's resting comfortably, albeit she was a bit feisty. I had to beat some sense into her."

Somehow, Lynn was able to respond.

"…….ffffff." she whispered.

"Huh? What was that my dear?" She motioned with her head to come closer. He got close enough to hear her now.

"Fuck you."

He immediately slapped her across the face. He then pulled out his knife and took hold of her index finger.

"You know, maybe, I didn't make myself clear." He said, angrily, and with the knife positioned at the bottom of her index finger. Fear engulfed her eyes. She panicked uncontrollably.

"Now, are you going to be good?"

She nodded her head down rapidly. Her breathing remained quick.

"Ok…" A sinister smile formed on his mouth. Without notice he violently cut off her finger. Lynn screamed in agony.

He smiled.

"Sorry, I lied, hahahahahahaha. Don't worry, I'll get something to close that up. Are you going to obey now?"

"Yes!!" She cried out, still feeling the pain.

"Let that be a lesson for you. I will not tolerate *defiance!*"

4 Hours Earlier

"That, was truly inspiring girl, a performance worthy of praise."

"........" Lisa paused. Tears slowly dripped down her face.

"Hey, you ok?."

".......Can we go now? .....I have to get out of here."

"Yeah, it's going to be alright Lisa, I'm here for you." They proceeded to the warm-up room to gather up their personal belongings before exiting the building. As they came across the exit doors they were approached by Chris Monroe.

"Lisa, that was great, you really stole the show." He could see the tears running down her cheeks. "Are you ok? What happened?"

Lynn intervened.

"It's been a long day for her, you know, what happened to her mother."

"Shit, I'm such an idiot, I didn't mean to..."

"Chris, it's ok alright, I just...I need some space right now." Lisa replied.

"Yeah, no, I understand, let me walk with you." In agreement, they headed to Lisa's car in the back parking lot. It was a quiet night. The winds were calm, but lurking was a terrible evil. As they neared her car, out of the bushes came a masked woman, wearing all black. Within seconds she had already pricked Lisa in the neck with the syringe. Almost immediately, she fell unconscious. After seeing this, Chris instantly tried to help her and struck the assailant in the back of the head. The masked woman turned around and hit him in the face with a pair of brass knuckles. He hit the ground hard. He thought he saw both girls knocked out and being placed in a blue van. The windows had been tinted, so he couldn't get a good look at the woman who took them.

—⟪⟫—

Jamie remained awake and silent, thinking about the emotional toll that had to be weighing on Ray. She had found some macaroni salad in a little fridge in the corner of the room. At least she wouldn't starve to death. Outside, a black Mercedes Benz had pulled up in front of McPherson's residence. Through the windows, five men armed with silenced weapons could be seen by a concerned citizen who quickly retreated back to his home. One of these men donned a thick, white beard with dark brown eyes. This man was Drake Winters. Winters flicked the switch on his lighter and gradually lit his cigarette. That was the signal to get out of the car. The four subordinates hurried to the front door and lined up, two on each side. The faint footsteps were silent to Jamie, but she could hear the loud bang after Winters kicked down the door. She entered defensive mode and pulled out her nine millimeter underneath her right sock. She found a silencer tucked in her jacket, which lay on the couch. Once screwed in, she found an area of the room shielded from sight and pressed her back against the wall. Drake came across the mechanism that controlled the basement door. He had received Intel from Reaper that allowed him to punch in the correct code. (Lisa's birth date) Jamie could hear the sound of the door open. She looked at her watch, it was 1:17A.M.

Riker's jeep was seen parked a few feet from his home. Seeing the open door and the armed squad, he walked towards them while loading his shotgun. One of the men saw him coming inside and took a shot at him. Riker tilted his head to avoid the bullet and instantly fired a shot directly through the man's chest. The impact carried his body against the wall and startled the rest of the men walking down the stairs. As the two in front turned their heads, Jamie rolled sideways out her hiding space and put three bullets in the closest one to the bottom and four in the one next to him. Every shot center mass.

"*Bitch!*" yelled Drake Winters as he shot three at her that Jamie swiftly dodged. At the same time another blistering round from the shotgun was heard, tearing through the final pour soul's skull. This left only Winters.

"*Put the fucking gun down!!*" yelled Riker.

I looked in his eyes and saw them wide and shocked. Immediately he dropped his weapon to the floor.

"*Jamie!*, you ok down there?"

"Yeah, considering." Jamie responded, now with her gun aimed at Winters as well.

"What do you want to do with him?" Jamie asked.

"Oh, I have a couple ideas. Now comes the fun part asshole." We guided him to the kitchen table.

"Cuff his ankles to the chair. Hold him there while I get the wood clamps."

"Wood clamps?" Jamie asked with a concerned look on her face.

I made my way down the basement and located two metal clamps, originally used for holding and securing boards of wood. I began to ask myself what evil was I about to unleash. Really, torturing him to acquire information I already knew was pointless. It came to me you see. While investigating the case a couple months ago, it had led me to an old, abandoned warehouse just ten miles from Queens. On the walls were images depicting satanic rituals and vicious mutilations that had Reaper's face plastered all over them. On the ceiling, large hooks dangled in front of me. Investigating further, I made my way down the empty halls and saw a cell door with vile instruments on the metal tables. I imagined that's where Lisa was being held. This was about all the women Winters ever maimed. He must not survive on this day. When I returned to the kitchen Jamie was shocked at what she saw.

"What the fuck are you doing?"

"Pull his wrists out."

"*What?!*"

"*Do it Jamie, Now!!*"

"You're not seriously going to do what he says, are you?" Winters asked in protest, hoping she would agree with him.

"*Shut up mother fucker!!*" Jamie yelled. I abruptly snapped his wrists into the clamps.

I pulled out my knives from their holsters. I forced them through his hands. Blood splashed out his skin as he screamed in agony.

"*How does it feel? To know you're at death's door and helpless to escape?*"

"Fuck you.......I ain't telling you shit. Lisa is going to die......heh, heh, heh."

I grabbed his hair and pulled back his head in furious response. I slipped a third knife through my sleeve and placed it horizontally against his throat.

"That's good to hear, because I already know where she is. This is the part where I watch you die for your sins." With those menacing words I ripped through his skin, slitting his throat, and slammed his head against the table.

"Jesus." Jamie replied in shock.

"Come on, help me clean this up."

"Riker, you know where she is?"

"Yeah, it's time to end this." I felt the demon clawing and ripping through my essence, the transformation was almost complete.

Lisa was crouched in the corner of the wall. Her clothes were torn with bruises around her visible skin. Her bottom lip was bleeding and a gash ran down her forehead. Startling, even more so than her wounds, was the way her eyes remained, as if infected by the curse her father laid down on her. It was the undying thirst for retribution, and the unquenchable desire of a broken soul. The same blood as her father flowed through her veins like a blistering volcano. Lisa McPherson wasn't backing down from the fight. She welcomed it with open arms.

3:15 A.M.

Trapped in this prison Lisa began to question her own sanity. Withstanding the beatings was easy, feelings of hopelessness was an entirely different story. She shed so much blood her body became like wet clay, weak and fragile. So many times she wanted to give up and die in her cell. Something, however, kept her from doing so, her father. She knew he'll come for her; he'll go through hell to save her. The very thought kept her from giving up.

"Mother fucker! You'll pay for this, you hear me?!! You'll pay for this, all of you!!" She screamed into the air, hoping they'd hear her. Suddenly,

four guards approached her cell with a purpose. They glared at her with anger. Without saying a word the man in front unlocked Lisa's cage and violently grabbed her by the arm.

"You're coming with us; Mr. Reaper wants a word with you."

"Let go of her!" Lynn yelled.

"Move!" the guard shouted. She was literally dragged down the decrepit hallway until she reached the Plexiglas chamber. A steel table was positioned in the center of the room. Attached to it were four metallic restraints. Unable to struggle from their grasp they placed her on the table and fastened the restraints to her wrists and ankles. To her right she saw Reaper remove a long tubular device from a bucket. Attached to the end of it lay a soaked rag with a large extension cord wrapped around it. Lisa could see the sparks begin to fly uncontrollably. Terror seeped through her veins but she remained steadfast. Reaper tore her shirt off to increase the level of pain. She winced in freight as a large smile erupted on his face.

"This will teach you some manners." He forced the rag on her stomach.

Lisa could feel the electricity ripple through her body.

"Ahhhhhhhhhhhhhhhhhhhhhhhhhhhhhhhh!" She screamed in agonizing pain. He held it there for a minute and released the rag from her skin. Lisa grinded her teeth in anger while breathing heavily. She didn't allow herself to be fazed. Lisa looked directly in Reaper's eyes with that same unbridled rage. Letting her ego get the best of her she began to laugh.

"Heh heh heh heh, is that the best you can do? Come oooooooon!!" In response he gladly placed the rag on her stomach again.

Lisa's screams echoed throughout the room in what seemed like an eternity. An hour had passed before she lost consciousness. When she came to Lisa found herself alone in a dark room. Her head rung continuously. She vomited on the floor. Lisa drifted to a troubled sleep. She didn't know how much more she could take. Lisa desperately needed a plan of escape or she would soon find herself at death's door.

3:36A.M.

In the jeep, tensions grew stronger and demon's danced in my head. I could hear their drums pounding away at my skull. Jamie couldn't get herself to look at me. She couldn't stop her hands from shaking. Could anyone blame her? She saw not her best friend, but a monster hell bent on destruction. I did my best to alleviate the current situation.

"Jamie..." she interrupted.

"There is nothing to talk about. I watched you butcher him without the slightest bit of hesitation."

"I know but..."

"No, you had no honor in it. I went along with it because I despised what he was, what he represented, but the look on your face, it was like the devil grabbed hold of your soul. It was slaughter, what happened at the mansion Ray? How many did you maim? Don't answer, cause I already know."

"They got what was coming to them. I became the reaper of evil. You can't imagine the power I felt, the utter freedom, no boundaries, no rules, nothing holding me back."

"Don't you understand? All you're doing is fueling the beast inside, until it completely consumes you."

"Sometimes, you have to become the beast, to defeat the monsters that roam the earth, regardless of circumstance. In the end, you can either accept it or you can't. We're here."

"This conversation isn't over." I looked at her.

"You ready?"

"Ready as I'll ever be."

Without blinking an eye, we loaded our firearms before entering the warehouse. Immediately upon entering with our weapons perched, the foul stench of rotting corpses made it's way through our nostrils.

"Fuck, what the hell happened in here?" Jamie asked.

"The usual, what you find in a sick man's lair. Be at your guard, I don't like this." It was worse than when I last saw it.

Looking in the rooms, we witnessed the savage mutilation of

humans. Organs hung from the hooks above. Walking further through the annals of hell, a sharp pain ripped through my head, almost triggering a sixth sense. Something horrible had just happened here. Moving closer to the source, it became far more heinous. As we reached the double doors in front of us, blood had seeped through the cracks below. We could hear the laughter of the sick fuck, relishing in his "accomplishment." At that moment, it was shoot first and ask questions later...no, I think just the killing was necessary. We looked at each other, thinking identically.

In a blaze of adrenaline we ferociously kicked down the doors. As soon as the cretin turned around we unloaded eighteen bullets into his body, creating a beautiful, blood smeared corpse. I saw in front of me a very much dead Lynn Sinclair. Pieces of her heart, already placed in her mouth, and her eyes, ripped from their sockets. Jamie threw up.

"Jesus Jamie, again? Hold it together."

"Fuck you, who is it?"

"Lynn Sinclair, my daughter's friend, closest friend. She didn't deserve this, no one does."

"Ray, you better take a look at this."

"What is it?" Jamie pointed to the closest side of the wall. It was yet another message from Reaper.

TOO LATE

MEET ME WHERE

IT ALL BEGAN

"Where it all began?" asked Jamie.

"You know the place Jamie. It's all connected. The island, íle da le mort." Jamie cringed.

"The Scarred Man, he is Desmond Reaper."

Fear can be described as a reaction to a heightened state of anxiety or intense series of anarchy. Perhaps, even simpler, fear results from even the slightest form of darkness, so intense as to create a severe shock through every molecule in the human body. We all fear one thing or another, it's merely inevitable. For me, it's fearing thy own self, that alone is a battle that cannot be won or conquered. A battle where there are no enemies but the demon inside your soul, and a demon that cannot be persuaded by righteousness or morality.

Once relieved of her blindfold, Lisa saw before her a beautiful Asian woman, dressed in black silk with a red cloth across her nose and mouth. Her mere presence was intimidating enough, but those eyes, captivating and terrifying at the same time; an intoxicating jade. Unsure of her motives, Lisa could not allow herself to trust this stranger. Reiyiko Lee Chang gazed into Lisa's eyes and licked her upper lip. Dazed and confused, Lisa could not predict what came next. Reiyiko ran towards her and emphatically slammed both hands on the wall, surrounding her face. Reiyiko's head rested on her's while she looked feverishly into her eyes. Lisa tried to contain her fear the best she could, but once she felt Reiyiko's tongue slither across her cheek and the bridge of her nose, she winced.

"*You're mine.*" Reiyiko whispered before kissing Lisa on the lips.

"Having fun are we?" Reaper asked.

"She's a good one, I can smell her fear, but I think there's more than meets the eye, perhaps a quiet rage."

"If she tries anything, do me a favor, don't kill her, not yet anyway. I want an audience after all." Reiyiko looked at him a bit disappointed.

"For you, as always."

"That's my girl." Lisa might have appeared weak and fragile, but little did they know, she was only buying time, looking for an opening. Risk often met with foolhardiness, however. She couldn't afford any mishaps, the stakes were just too high.

We decided to meet up at Jamie's place. As the doors opened I saw before me a vast array of weapons that were hung on the walls. On the table to the left, various knives were neatly placed. Hanging from the ceiling lay a pair of beautiful Katana blades in their pristine sheaths.

"Ah, the Katanas. Brings me back Blade."

"Blade, that's what you guys called me. Gotta say I still love the name. Riker, I need to know your mind is clear, this darkness of yours, I fear the worst."

"What about you? You talk about the darkness within me, but I know what you went through on that island, what you needed to do to survive. You of all people should understand."

"What I did on that island, I never want to experience again. I keep on seeing The High King in my mind, haunting me. I killed him, and the horrible Chef, but it hasn't erased the pain. I think about it, every day."

"You don't have to like it J, but it's all I have left. Lisa is the only thing that matters now. Come on, it's time to make the call."

3:55A.M.

FBI Special Agent Mai Wu Long heard her cell phone vibrating and pressed on the send button. To her right was her Boss, Avery Jackson.

"Hello?"

"Mai, it's me, we got a situation."

"Jamie O'Neil." She replied somewhat worrisome. "What's going on?"

"You know about that serial killer running loose? Who does he remind you of?" Dread filled Mai's heart.

"Yes, the scarred man Reiyiko mentioned."

"That bastard murdered Amanda, and now he has Lisa. We're bringing the team back together."

"I'll put a call in to Laura and Sam."

"Good, tell them to meet up at my place." Mai hung up.

"Going back to hell are we?" asked Avery.

"Here we go again."

"Let's do this Shell Shock, for Lisa." Avery said.

—⟋⟍—

Lisa sat, staring at Reiyiko with stern eyes. Reiyiko merely grinned at her prisoner like a predator stalking its prey, but this prey was a formidable adversary, tenacious and volatile. The fear she experienced earlier had all but vanished. She looked on, unfazed by her captor. When she saw that Reaper had left the room, Lisa thought an opportunity presented itself. If she was going to escape and call for help, she needed to get Reiyiko's attention, get her up close. At that moment, Lisa slowly stood up, using the wall as leverage. This peaked Reiyiko's curiosity, as she walked toward Lisa while removing her dagger from it's sheath. This terrified Lisa momentarily but she was committed to the strategy. Reiyiko moved in close and toyed with her captor.

"Now now, what is it that you're up to my dear?" Reiyiko asked.

"Up to? I have no idea what you're talking about, I'm just stretching my legs."

Reiyiko didn't buy it.

"*Liar!* You're up to something....... don't do anything stupid *little Geishan.*" She pressed the blade against Lisa's face, dragging it closer to her left eye.

"*Or I'll snatch it right out.*" Lisa felt a strange calmness take over her. She didn't feel the blade at all.

Reiyiko, still curious of her captive's intentions, stared at her with much patience. After what felt like an eternity, Reiyiko slowly placed the dagger back in its sheath. When Reiyiko turned away from Lisa, the adrenaline kicked in and she forcefully swung Reiyiko around with her free legs and delivered a head-butt directly to her face. Lisa attempted to run to a nearest exit but found herself fall hard against the floor. Reiyiko had violently tripped Lisa with a double sweep kick. The only thing she saw next was a fist coming toward her and then darkness.

Lisa groggily started to come to, her vision blurred, trying to make out her surroundings. At first she felt cold and slowly realized her shirt and pants had been removed. With urgency rifling through her, she tried to move but felt resistance from her body. Something was pushing her arms and legs down. She looked to her left and right and found that her wrists were tied down to what appeared to be a cross. She then looked down and found that her ankles were restrained as well.

"Well, well, it seems the young lioness has awoken. I take it you may be wondering, what is it that we have planned for you." Reaper said with malicious intent. Lisa snapped back.

"Kiss my ass you perverted fuck, why don't you just kill me already?"

"Oh come now Lisa, if you want to die so badly I'll gladly grant your request, but not until your father gets here. After all, what better way to break a man than seeing his own daughter murdered and realizing there was nothing he could do to stop it. As Jesus felt, nailed to that cross in the beating sun, pleading for help, desperately calling out for his Father to save him, but He did not intervene, He just left his own son there, to die. I know, not exactly the same situation. Unlike God, your father will at least attempt to save you, cause that's the kind of man he is. Tell me, does it frighten you, to die, knowing your father failed to keep his word?"

"Fuck you. My father, when he comes, whatever plans you have for him, no matter how hard you try, even if I'm dead before he gets here, he'll still kill you all."

"Such confidence Lisa, I like that, too bad it won't matter in the end."

"When do we get to kill her? I want to be the one that does it, please baby, I want to see his face when I slit her throat." Replied Reiyiko.

"Anything for you my dear, nothing would please me more."

—m—

"Ahhhhhhh!" Lisa screamed as the whip slashed hard against her stomach, ripping into her skin. Again and again, the whip shredded her skin, blood seeping down her body. As the next strike came, she couldn't help but grin at Reiyiko in defiance. She refused to scream any longer.

Reiyiko grabbed Lisa by the throat.

"Bitch! Grin all you want, you won't be smiling when I'm done with you." Lisa spit in her face.

"Bring it on."

Reiyiko punched her in the face and removed her Katana blade. Without mercy, Reiyiko sliced off a couple of her fingers, gushing out blood. Lisa screamed in agony. Afterward, Reiyiko bandaged her wound up to stop the bleeding, after all, she had to keep her alive.

"Reiyiko!!" Reaper yelled. *"What have you done?!!"*

"Relax Des, she was just being a little *cunt*, had to teach her a lesson."

"No more surprises. We must be prepared."

Lisa could hear the van coming to a stop, which slowed down her breathing. Almost accustomed to the mask, she felt no need to hyperventilate. The doors opened up, and she could hear the shouts and commands from her captors, followed by the physical grabbing as they pulled her out of the vehicle. After five minutes of walking blindfolded, she could hear a plane's engine running. They abruptly threw her inside. Their destination was île de la mort.

—m—

Part III: Consequences

McBride Residence

The shower was running as Laura McBride got the call from Mai Wu Long. Her gear and weapons were already packed in a black duffle bag. She entered the bathroom and slowly got undressed before stepping into the shower. As she was getting ready, a car had parked near her residence. A young man stepped out of the vehicle wearing a mask. He peered up at the top window that had the light on. He smiled within his mask as he moved closer, hearing the water fall from the shower. Another beautiful woman to add to his list of victims. He was smart, his crimes were kept under the radar, too much attention was focused on Desmond Reaper, his master. As he got closer to the window, he could see a good glimpse of the purple haired girl. She wasn't his favorite, whom he had tasted so many years ago on that island, but she was delectable nonetheless.

He moved slowly to the back door, where he silently began picking the lock with his tools. Laura didn't hear him enter the house. The intruder slowly ascended the stairs up to her bedroom and waited. After a few more minutes, he could hear the water stop as Laura started to dry up. As this was happening, the masked man removed the sleeping powder from his pocket. Laura wrapped the towel around her waist, careless to cover her top as she believed to be in privacy. The intruder got into position, doing his best to keep out of her radar. As she was about to enter the bedroom, however, a feeling went through her head, as if triggering a sixth sense. She was not alone. "Shit." she said to herself. Knowing her weapons were out of reach, she went to grab her shaving razor. Unfortunately, the intruder also sensed her movements and burst into the door. The sleeping powder found its mark as Laura quickly fell unconscious. The intruder reveled in his victory and slowly bent down toward her. He gracefully untied her towel. He licked her navel before carrying her to the bed. Placing her on the bed he began his routine, groping and sucking upon every inch of her. The time came to take out the carving tool. With a grin plastered on his face he whispered in her ear.

"You're mine bitch, time to die." With those words he plunged the blade in her heart. She gurgled in shock as death took hold of her. Her tongue creeped out of her mouth as he dragged the knife down to her navel. Once complete, he took out a large body bag and placed it on the floor. He then put Laura's corpse inside. Afterward he ventured off to his hideout where a plane was waiting for him.

Ray and Jamie waited patiently for the team to show up, unaware of the recent tragedy that had befallen Laura. Shortly after, they heard the humming of a motorcycle, followed by a Ford F-350 that parked in the driveway. Mai removed her helmet and made her way to the front door. From the truck emerged Avery Jackson, just as big as before. I opened the door and greeted them with enthusiasm.

"Shell Shock." I said.

"Riker, talk about De Ja Vu." Mai stated.

I smiled and looked past her to my good friend Avery Jackson.

"Bone-Crusher, you know you still owe me fifty bucks right?" Bone-Crusher gave me a look of confusion.

"Fifty bucks? And why would I possibly owe you?"

"What, you don't remember? The fucking bet?"

"I have no idea what the *fuck* you're talking about bra."

"Allow me to refresh your memory. You bet me fifty bucks that Seth Rollins was gonna win the triple threat match, does it ring a bell now?"

"*Mother fucker*, that was a *travesty*, how could they disrespect my boy like that? Furthermore, there was no hand shake, the bet has no validity."

"*What the fuck?* Of course we shook hands man, you just don't want to admit it. It's all part of your sick obsession with Rollins, what, do you want to *marry* the guy? He's fucking overrated."

"*Overrated! Blasphemy!*"

"*Boys, boys!* Can we get back to business here, my *God*, giving me a headache." Replied Jamie.

"Alright, alright, you still owe me fifty bucks though."

Jamie jumped in before Avery could bite back.

"*Save it!* We're going after Lisa, remember? Ray, what the hell is the matter with you?"

"Yes, as always your right Jamie, but I haven't forgotten." Avery changed his mood.

"Nor have I my friend. This is what's important." I gave him a nod.

"Hey, where are Sam and Laura? I was just on the phone with Laura half an hour ago. Weird they'd be late." replied Mai.

Concern ran through our minds.

"Yeah, and Sam too, what could be taking them?" asked Jamie.

—⚏—

Sam Rivers woke up to darkness, his eyes covered with a black cloth. He couldn't remember what had happened. One minute, he was driving to Jamie's, the next minute, nothing. He then started thinking again. It was an ambush, someone had derailed him off the road. Now the feeling was different, as if he were in a plane. His breathing remained calm, bracing himself for the events to come. Out of nowhere, he felt the excruciating pain of being hit with a steel chain. Again and again, the strikes came down hard on his back and chest. His assailants didn't bother to remove his blindfold and continued the vicious assault, shredding his skin. Sam could do nothing as he felt resistance from his restraints that hung from the ceiling of the plane. It seemed like the torture lasted forever, but finally it stopped. At that moment his assailants finally removed his blind fold. What he saw looking back at him was terrifying. It was Laura's head, her face contorted awkwardly with her tongue hanging down her mouth. Fury erupted in his veins like a sweltering hot cauldron. Holding her head in front of him was none other than the young apprentice from those days long ago. He had a big smile on his face. Just then the cretin spoke.

"Oh, what's the matter, was she your girlfriend or something? I remember seeing you in the crowd, right before your team *slaughtered my brothers and sisters!*" With that he punched Sam in the face.

"Murderers, all of you, especially this little *cunt!*" The apprentice put her head back in front of him.

"What a punk, with that colorful hair. I had to teach her a lesson. She was very beautiful though. The look on her face was priceless before I put her to sleep, and that body, that sweet delicious body. She tasted like honey."

"*Mother fucker!! I'm gonna fucking kill you!!*" The apprentice tossed Laura's head to the side and grabbed Sam by the face.

"And her heart, like the cherry on top, I can still taste it. Don't worry though, soon you will have a chance to join her, *in hell.*" The blind fold was placed back on him. Their destination was île de la mort.

—✕—

"Something's wrong. I don't like this guys." said Jamie.

"Yeah, I got a bad feeling too, but we have to get going, there's no time to stick around." replied Avery. The team in full agreement, they headed down to the helipad where Trisha Mills was waiting for them.

"Yo guys, what's up? Hey, where the hell are Laura and Sam?" Trisha asked.

"No idea, and that's the scary part, but we can't wait." I said.

"Shit, OK, I'll get you there as soon as possible."

"Wait, do you hear something?" I said. Abruptly, a bullet tore through Trisha's head, splashing out blood. Shock overtook the team. Before they could react, they were all pricked in the necks with tranquilizer darts. In the darkness, Riker could see a figure in the distance. It was a red silhouette, outlined in flame.

Part IV: Winchester

Sam's gear and weapons were being distributed amongst the group. He was dragged down a lengthy tunnel of mud and dirt. He was then thrown down several feet into a massive cage. Sam shook off the pain from the fall and slowly stood up. The cage was built to be an arena. Instead of metal bars, however, it was constructed completely out of barbed wire. He noticed the circle he was standing in was outlined in red. They had held on to the traditions of the Cannibal Horde that was decimated a decade ago. Obviously they improved things since then. Sam scanned the arena, spotting several passageways surrounding him. He heard movement emanating from every one of them. Sam prepared himself for a fight. His opponents emerged from the darkness, armed to the teeth with brass knuckles, steel chains, and sledgehammers. There had to be at least twenty of them, staring daggers into him.

Sam realized at that moment, there was no coming back from this one. Death was in sight, but Sam figured if he was to die, he would gladly take down as many as he could. Just as soon as that thought crossed his mind, it began. They decided to take their time. Five of them rushed at him with vigor. Sam intercepted the first one with a side block against his arm, before pummeling him with a straight kick to his stomach that sent the man careening into two of them. When he did, another attempted to whip at his chest with a chain. Before it could make contact, he stepped inward and grabbed hold of a chunk of it, twisting it securely against his arm. He aggressively pulled it back, carrying the man with him and thrust his knee into his face. Blood shot out of his mouth. Sam was then struck in the face with a set of brass knuckles, cutting away his cheek and chin. He fell to his knees and was hit again with the brass knuckles, rattling his skull.

Sam was resilient though, rolling out of the way of a sledgehammer attack. He sprung back up and tackled his opponent to the ground, reigning down fists upon his face. The attack was short lived as he felt a chain constrict around his throat. Tighter and tighter the grip became, restricting his airways. While he was losing his breath, one of them thrust a sledgehammer against his abdomen. He coughed up blood in agony. Another strike bombarded his stomach, the pain surging up his spine. Just when it seemed the chain suffocating him would put him down for good, the grip loosened, eventually releasing its hold. He could already tell the reason why. This was meant to be a humiliation, they wanted him to suffer. The rest of the pack joined in, hammering away at him until he was left bloodied and broken. Weak from the assault, a loud cry from a horn echoed throughout the arena. The pack moved away from their victim in response. Out from the shadows appeared The Apprentice. He walked toward Sam, clapping his hands.

"Bravo Mr. Rivers, bravo. You lasted a mere three minutes, astonishing. I honestly thought you had more life left in you."

Sam snapped back.

"*Fuck you.*"

"Hahaha, quite pathetic. I would kill you myself, but watching you get torn limb from limb by my friends here would be far more satisfying. Think of it this way, now you get to join that cocky little whore of yours. Have at him boys." As The Apprentice was walking away, the combatants converged on Sam. Moving closer to him, he began to laugh uncontrollably. This intrigued The Apprentice, who halted the group's advancement.

"*Heheheheh, I'll see you all in hell.......for Raven.*" The Apprentice's eyes turned to horror as he heard the clicks of the grenades that Sam lay hidden beneath his belt.

"I love you Laura." Sam whispered. Three seconds later the explosion annihilated the entire arena. The force from the impact flung The Apprentice far across a dirt hall, sending him sliding into the back wall. Rising slowly afterward, The Apprentice learned the dangers of underestimating his enemies. Despite the loss of his men, he creaked a smile. His enemies were down to four. The master will be pleased.

Part V: Shell Shock

Mai Wu Long opened her eyes to steel bars. She could feel the hot air penetrate her ears. She knew exactly where she was, angered by the manner in which she was brought here. Desmond Reaper had been tracking the team for years, somehow escaping their radar, but how, she thought to herself. How could he have known their identities all this time? A horrifying thought sent shockwaves through her mind. There was only one way he could have known. Someone close to them leaked out the information. Then it hit her, cold and hard. It was Reiyiko Lee Chang. She saw her getting on a boat with Reaper on that day. It was after the team found Bruce dead. Ray and Rachel were left unconscious. When he came to, Ray had told her he was hit from behind with what felt like a rock and earlier, Reiyiko was following their trail. What she couldn't understand was why? Why would her best friend escape with her tormentor? It didn't make any sense. Mai knew she was unpredictable, but to succumb to evil? No, she refused to believe it. There had to be more to it, she thought, desperately searching for a good reason.

October 6th, 1992

This had to have been the twentieth time that Mai Wu Long entered the psychiatric ward to visit her friend. The feeling was often always the same, cold and unsettling. It felt claustrophobic walking through the white halls before entering the main visitation quarters. More and more, it seemed like Reiyiko had lost a part of her soul, unable to display any hints of happiness. She tried for weeks to make her smile, to try and release the darkness still attached to her. Mai could tell she was still shaken after her parents tried to kill her. Her parents left her all alone, forced to spend her days trapped like a wounded animal. Of course she would be closed out from the world after facing constant abuse. She hoped the current visit would bring them back to the good times they shared together, keeping the past buried out of sight. Mai immediately smiled when she sat down in front of her, offering her a rose.

"Reiyiko look, I found this rose in my backyard. I wanted to give it to you. I remembered how much you loved the smell of them."

Reiyiko barely showed any emotion. Her words were quiet and monotone.

"I'm sorry Mai, but I am no longer attached to these dainty little trinkets."

"Oh come on Reiyiko, you don't have to be such a sad sap, I know you." Reiyiko suddenly snapped at her, taking Mai aback.

"*I don't want your stupid rose!!*" Reiyiko grabbed the rose from her and crinkled it up, before tossing it on the floor. Mai couldn't blame Reiyiko for her reaction, she just felt sorry for her. She quickly changed the subject.

"Ok, forget about the flower. I just want my best friend back, remember her? Despite all the things she endured, she always had a smile on her face whenever she saw me. All those times we stayed up late to watch horror movies or chilling at the local ice cream bars. I need that girl to come back to me."

"Believe me Mai, I'd like to pretend that I'm that same girl, full of life and happiness. Now, now I see the truth. Now I see emptiness, only the dark. I murdered my parents. The *blood, all that blood,* covering me. *I can still see their faces, those dead faces,* a constant reminder of what I really am, a monster."

"No, you are not a monster. You had no other choice. How could you be accountable for their deaths? They put you in that position, you merely did what you had to survive."

"No, you don't understand. When I killed them, I felt euphoric, and I enjoyed it. I felt as though a weight was lifted. *It was manic, no remorse, no guilt.*"

"But that's understandable. After all the abuse you took, they never loved you. It's normal to feel emotional. Now you can move on with your life."

"*No damn it! Don't you get it!* There is no normal after that. All there is, *is suffering and pain.* Nothing else matters anymore."

"Don't say that Reiyiko. I can help you, have faith in me. Rid yourself of the darkness. Please, I'm begging you."

"I'm afraid it's too late for me Mai. The friend you know is dead." Tears streaked down Mai's face.

Present Day

Mai could hear movement coming her way. She stood up and placed her hands on the metal bars, gripping them tight. Her face became embedded with tension. She could sense Reiyiko's presence. From her peripheral, she saw her. She wore an orange Nunjitsu robe with a black belt around her waist. Her eyes and nose were painted over with streaks of black, her jade eyes still crystal clear. Now face to face, there existed a cold ripple between them. Each had changed dramatically from years past. Reiyiko was the first to speak.

"Well, well, we meet again at last old friend. What's the matter? Not happy to see me? *I'm shocked!*" Mai looked at her with venomous eyes.

"*Why Reiyiko?* Why would you do this? Tell me you had a good reason."

"Why? *Why?!! Of all people, you ask me that!* Reaper showed me the truth, he *accepted me!* When have you ever done that?" Her response startled Mai.

"*How can you say such things!* I *always accepted* you, who you really are. After everything we've been through, *the deaths, Julia, Amy!* How can you stand there and give favor to a *madman!!!*"

"*No!* He freed them. They were weak, of no consequence. He saw the spirit within me, *strong, and fierce, a worthy warrior.*"

"You can't possibly believe that. Where is this coming from? You told me you were repulsed by him, wanting nothing more than to see him *dead!*"

"That was before. It's true, I did loath him at first, after what he did to me, seeing my friends slaughtered in front of me. But I realized something. He was teaching me. He showed me what weakness brings, only depravity and death. It's the strong who prosper, who achieve enlightenment. When we feast on the weak, it redeems their souls and provides us nourishment. Everything becomes balanced. We became a family, and your team slaughtered them!"

"Oh my God. I can't believe what I'm hearing. *We were there to rescue you!!* There is nothing but evil on this island and it has clearly tainted your mind."

"Think what you want, it won't change anything, but you can still be redeemed Mai. You are strong, formidable. Join us and bask in all the wonders we provide."

"Never. I will never join you."

"Then you shall die like the rest. Now if you excuse me, I have another matter to attend to. Think about my offer." Reiyiko walked away.

Mai remained, frozen in heart break. Her best friend was dead, lost to insanity. Just then Reiyiko stopped in stride.

"By the way, I left a present for you in your cell. You'll need it for the test ahead." Confusion swept through Mai's face. She turned her head and saw her Sai's on the small ledge to her left. Out of curiosity, she gently pushed the cell door. It opened easily, and it occurred to her the real game was about to begin. She took the Sai's and walked down the illuminated hallway. The hallway led her down to a set of wooden doors. Bracing herself for what lurked beyond the doors, she took a deep breath. Opening the doors, she saw before her an array of combatants, each donning the paints of the cannibal horde. Mai entered the fray. Her opponents fanned out, looking for an opening to strike. Mai taunted her enemies, almost begging them to come up close. Roy did not take too kindly to that and engaged.

Mai welcomed the attack with furious stabs to the gut, before driving a Sai threw his throat. At the same time she countered Jeremy with a kick to the stomach, forcing him to the ground. The pace was quickening and volatile as yet another lunged at her with a pair of knives. Mai trapped the knives and twisted downward, giving her the opportunity to head-butt Charlie in the face. Jeremy got up and tried to take her off guard. She was ready for him. With lightning fast reflexes, she stabbed him in the left arm with one Sai, in the hand with the other. She then ripped out both Sai's and thrust them threw his eyes, squirting out blood. Within an instant she delivered an acrobatic spin in the air. While coming down she drove a Sai threw Charlie's head. Sensing more assailants, from her knees, she launched a Sai threw the next one's chest charging her from the right.

Suddenly, a machete came barreling towards her. She evaded the strike with a side roll and jarred him in the face with a blistering kick. As he was falling down she leapt on top of him and stabbed him in the upper thigh. At the same time she retrieved her other Sai and thrust it in his opposite thigh. Without mercy, she then tore out both weapons and angrily thrust them threw his throat. At that moment she screamed out.

"Reiyiko!! Show yourself!! Mai couldn't find her. She'd have to search.

Shattered Bond

Lisa McPherson was stirring, her body still torn from the whip. A bandage was wrapped around the space where her two severed fingers used to be. Reiyiko had dressed her with an old faded crop top and shorts. Her feet remained bare. She had also painted a black streak across her eyes, with a singular red flame positioned just above her navel. She was surrounded by the same outlined circle that was used in the dreaded death pits. Unlike the previous battles, there were no spectators. Just then, Lisa could hear a familiar voice in the background.

"Lisa McPherson, how fitting we come together again." Lisa slowly pulled herself to her feet. Anger spread across her face when she spoke.

"Reiyiko. What is this? *Haven't you had enough!*"

"Oh come now Lisa, you brought it all upon yourself. It was because of your defiance that you stand here."

"*Fuck you, I won't stop. I will never give up.*"

"*Yes!* Such strong words. I admire your tenacity and your fighting spirit. You will need all of it. You are standing in the death pit, a test of will and strength. Normally, If you were to pass, you would join the ranks of the death squad, strong and ruthless. Unfortunately, your father and his allies saw fit to slaughter them all. As punishment for that egregious offense, you will join them in death and your body shall be feasted upon like the days of old."

"You're sick."

Reiyiko smiled in response.

"Look at it this way my dear. You have the distinct honor of facing me, Reaper's deadliest of servants. Your death shall be magnificent. However, since I like you, I will give you the opportunity to strike first. *Show me your rage!*" Reiyiko stepped into the circle and stopped in the middle. Directly in front of Lisa, she put her hands behind her back and leaned her head up close. Lisa's fist clenched, sweat ran down her face.

"You asked for it." She waited at first, until unloading all her strength in her fist. She swung with such velocity that the impact rocked Reiyiko to the ground. She spit out saliva from her mouth and wiped it off her chin. Reiyiko started to laugh.

"Heheheheh, not bad, not bad, but I'm afraid that'll be the only advantage you get." Reiyiko gradually got back up as Lisa braced herself for the attack.

Before she got a chance, Lisa quickly swung first, but Reiyiko swiftly dodged it and derailed her with an uppercut to the face. Lisa spat out blood. Reiyiko immediately followed that with a bone-rattling kick to the side of her ribs. Lisa clutched her ribs in pain as she fell to her knees, but there was no respite. Reiyiko picked her up by her shirt and savagely head-butted her in the face. Not done, she head-butted her in the face a second time, dropping Lisa to the ground. She began coughing up blood, her body already spent. As Reiyiko saw her there, laid out and dazed, an eerie smirk appeared on her face. She bent down and kissed Lisa's navel before mounting on top of her stomach. Peering into Lisa's eyes she spoke.

"You're mine." One fist careened against her face, and then another. They continued to come down hard, it seemed to never end. Then it stopped. Bloody and broken, Lisa was still breathing. After a brief pause, Reiyiko rose her hands up in the air and formed a massive fist. Lisa could barely see anything at all, only shades of white. She knew it would be over soon and readied herself.

"Reiyikooooooooo!!!!" Mai screamed. The scream halted her progress. Lisa was given a respite as Reiyiko's attention turned toward Mai.

"*Get away from her!* It's me you want. I challenge you in the death pit." Reiyiko smirked.

"I accept." She looked down at Lisa.

"It seems you get to live Lisa. Lucky little Geishan." Reiyiko dragged Lisa out of the circle before kicking her in the face, knocking her unconscious. It enraged Mai, who slowly walked toward the circle, her Sai's held firm. Reiyiko stepped back in and waited in anticipation. Mai stopped in front of her and drew daggers into her eyes.

Just then, Mai tossed a Sai down at Reiyiko's feet.

"We do this right, so there can be no dispute."

Reiyiko satisfied with the suggestion, picked up the Sai with enthusiasm.

"I must say Mai, I like your style. It's a shame it comes down to this. *I will truly mourn your death!*"

"We shall see."

The combatants circled around each other, looking for an opportunity to strike. It was not a battle that either of them foresaw, for that it was truly tragic. Hesitation settled in, before they lunged at each other with Sai's, both colliding together, glistening in a stand still. They retracted them and struck down low, clanging against each other once more. Their fierceness grew as the battle deepened. Each Sai seemed to connect with every attack, showcasing the wielder's skill. They were evenly matched, neither backing down. A moment of pause stopped the frenzy as they eyed each other intently, without a word spoken.

Then it began again, the Sai's clashing once more at the middle. This time, Mai was able to trap the Sai and twist it downward. The move slightly tweaked Reiyiko's wrist, giving Mai the opening to head-butt her in the face. As Reiyiko was falling back, Mai moved the Sai outward and lunged her knee into her stomach. She followed that up with a blistering punch to the face, knocking her Sai out of her hand. As Reiyiko fell, she used her quick reflexes and tripped Mai to the ground with a sweep kick. That was followed with a front kick to the face, shooting out blood. With Mai down, she immediately pulled her up by the hair and clamped her hands against her neck like a Boa-constrictor, squeezing tightly. Mai's eyes bulged as she felt the air being cut off from her lungs. The more she struggled, the harder Reiyiko squeezed. Mai, who still held on to her Sai like a vice, used it to break free, stabbing Reiyiko in the thigh. Reiyiko grimaced in pain and attempted to remove it. Before she could, Mai delivered a side kick to her stomach, sending her crashing to the ground. When Mai started to advance toward her, Reiyiko spotted her fallen Sai close to her. She quickly snatched it up and shielded it from sight. As Mai went to grab her, Reiyiko spun around and abruptly thrust it in the side of Mai's stomach. Mai's eyes turned to shock as blood dripped down her body. She couldn't believe she missed it. She fell down to her knees, grabbing hold of the edge of the Sai. Reiyiko grew a smirk, leaning in close.

"I win." She said with piercing clarity. Suddenly though, Mai as if possessed, ripped the Sai out of her stomach and plunged it deep into Reiyiko's lung. She desperately gasped for air, the pierce of the blade suffocating her. Mai slowly pulled the other Sai out of Reiyiko's thigh. She grabbed the back of her hair. She pulled her head back and positioned the Sai in front of her throat. A single tear flowed down Mai's face before she spoke.

"I'm sorry." The blade slowly penetrated Reiyiko's throat, blood raining down. Reiyiko could do nothing but stare up at her with terrified eyes. Tears began to flow down her cheeks as well. Eventually she fell to the ground, letting out her final breath. Mai, looking down at her body, paused briefly, before she too, collapsed down to the ground. With little strength she had within her, she crawled her way toward Lisa, who was still unconscious. Then she laid back down, fading to unconsciousness. Before she did, however, she saw a figure coming towards them. Blackness overcame her.

Part VI: Blade

Blood exited Jamie's mouth as her face felt the effects of the brass knuckles. Cuts and bruises were revealed on her cheek bones and below her eyes. Reaper grew a smirk on his face as he punished his captive. Wanting to humiliate her even more he tore her shirt off and in a perverted way, licked her stomach.

"My my, I have to tell you Jamie, that felt good. Now, here's a little present I've been meaning to give you. Consider it my welcoming card." He kissed her navel and viciously punched her in the stomach.

The force caused more blood to spew from her mouth.

"Oh I'm sorry, did that hurt? You're so beautiful... when you're in pain." Jamie didn't give Reaper the satisfaction he desperately wanted. She slowly turned her head, looked him in the eyes, and spit in his face. Reaper, angry now, wiped the spit off with his handkerchief and turned his attention to the cattle prod that had been sitting in a hot glaze.

"That was a big mistake my dear, it's time you felt the full extent of my ability." He reached for the cattle prod and aimed it at her abdomen. Jamie knew what was coming next so she tried to suck it up and prepare herself. Unfortunately, the pain she was about to experience was too excruciating to bear. Once the prod reached her abdomen her scream echoed throughout the room.

"Doesn't feel too good does it? Oh, but I can do even better than that." With pure malice he placed the cattle prod on her thigh. The results remained the same. There was no telling how much longer she could withstand the punishment. Not satisfied at all he placed the prod on her opposite thigh. Jamie screamed again, only this time, after that moment of pain she began to laugh at her captor.

Reaper snapped at her.

"And what's so funny, you bitch!"

"Heh, heh, heh, it won't matter, none of it will matter."

"What are you talking about?"

"Oh Reaper, you're really quite pathetic….. is this how you get..*your kicks*. You like to beat up young women? *I got news for you, I like pain.*"

"Save the tough girl act. Look at you, I've stripped you of your dignity."

"Enjoy your little peep show, but make no mistake; *He,* will not stop until the last thing you see in this life….is a pool of your own blood."

"Well, we'll just see about that, as for you, it's time to go to sleep." With that he delivered a hellacious head-butt that knocked her out.

Unsettled Score

As she came to, Jamie noticed she was fitted with a ragged crop top and shorts. As she looked up she caught sight of a horrifying scene. It was her good friend and ally Laura McBride, dissected like an animal. Her head lay impaled on a pike. Her body parts were piled up underneath. Such a vile image, she vomited on the ground. Tears streaked down her face as she could barely speak. Then, she heard it. That voice, that slimy voice, once again slithering through her ears. All that time ago, the perverted young man obsessed with her. She was utterly disgusted when she saw the sight of him. This time, he appeared bathed in the red paint of The Alpha, holding her Katana blades. Her rage burning up inside.

"Ahhhhh, we meet again my little flower. I must say, you haven't changed a bit, still as sexy as ever." Her voice cut the air.

"*Bastard!! What have you done!!*"

"Ohhhh this, was she your friend? So delicious, though not nearly as much as you. You, who are so very perfect, ripe and sweet. This one thought she was so bad, but I showed her. She was really quite pathetic in the end."

"And I bet you enjoyed every second. Tell me, how did you do it? It couldn't have been easy. I know Laura, no way she'd ever lose to you. Then again, you're not a *man*, no, *hell*, you're not even a *boy*, you're a *fucking cockroach*."

The Apprentice lashed out at her.

"*Hold your tongue bitch!*"

"*Ahhhh, what's the matter asshole, lose your balls?* I got it, you must have caught her off guard. In the shower right? *Yeah, that's something you'd do.* You don't have the *guts* to look a woman in the *face*. You crept up on her when she was finished, *didn't you?* Sprayed her with that smoke. That's the only reason you're still standing here."

"Bravo, you figured it out. What are you gonna do about it? Reaper did a number on you, all bruised up and bloody. Don't know why he had to abuse that belly though, that's a shame. Too bad I'll have to kill you. At least I'll get to dine on that scrumptious body of yours, bet it melts in my mouth."

"*Heh, you're sick, good, I like that, it only feeds my hate.* You know, I've always been known as the calm one, always the moral compass. *I'm gonna make an exception with you. I'm gonna make sure you die screaming.*"

The Apprentice readied the Katana's.

"I'll be getting those back by the way."

"I'd like to see you try." He responded. The Apprentice moved toward her in haste, looking to take advantage of her current state. Jamie prepared herself, unfazed. As the blades came down diagonal toward her body, she easily sidestepped to the right, tripping him in the process. As he started to lose his balance, she swiftly grabbed hold of one of her swords and ripped it from his grasp. Jamie smirked as he fell awkwardly to the ground, cutting his arm in the process. She teased him, waving her finger in front of his face. He glared at her in anger before rushing toward her. He swung at her aggressively, but was met with a block from her own. Consumed by rage, he started swinging at her wildly. She blocked each strike with ease, showcasing her skill.

Then she rushed him. With a surge of adrenaline, she grabbed his wrist and twisted it with her free hand, moving the sword away from her face. She reversed her blade with the other hand and jabbed the handle against his head. When he was falling backward, she pulled out the other sword from his hand. As he dropped to the ground she brutally kicked him in the face. She turned around, relishing in her accomplishment. She had regained her trusty Katana blades. Jamie allowed him to recover. She smirked at him.

"*Told you.* Now, allow me to show you why they really call me Blade." His reaction surprised Jamie. He started to laugh. Just then he was flanked by several men, armed with knives and basked in the markings of the Cannibal Horde.

"Kill her." There had to be at least twelve of them, coming at her like hungry wolves. She readied her swords for the attack. As the first one came in range, she swung her swords outward, deflecting the knives. Immediately, she thrust both blades through his stomach. Just as soon as she did, she retracted the blades, crisscrossed them in front of his throat, and cut his head off. Blood splashed everywhere. She kept in pace, driving a sword through the next man's chest coming at her from the right. At the same time, she blocked another to her left, before driving the sword in her opposite hand through his stomach. She followed suit by piercing his throat with both swords. Seconds after, she violently swung both swords diagonal, shredding through the next one's chest. In fluid motion, she crisscrossed her blades in front of her next opponent's waist. She followed through, tearing out flesh before slicing upward, severing his arms. He didn't scream for long as her blades impaled his eyes. Jamie never let up. Like a well-oiled machine, she bent down and chopped off another's ankles, spraying out blood. As he fell on his back, she lunged up in the air and drove the blades through his jaw. The Apprentice watched in terror as Jamie continued to maim his cohorts. The next one never stood a chance. She sliced through his stomach with one sword and cut off his head with the other. Her body was completely drenched in blood. Her wounds never seemed to bother her. Revenge for Laura fueled her determination. She adjusted her swords, slicing upward through the next one's throat. Her enemies were dwindling fast. Now only three remained, trying to figure out their next move. Jamie waited patiently, staring back at them with fire in her eyes. Two decided to rush at her, but they ran right into a buzz saw. She spun on her knees with her swords pointed outward, severing ankles and legs in the process. This cleared an opening for the last one, who dove at her with a machete. She quickly blocked the weapon with both swords and pushed herself up. Jamie went down low, kicking him hard in the groin. Collapsed down to his knees, she forced the blades through his chest. The two wounded men attempted to crawl away, but they didn't get far. Jamie noticed this and didn't hesitate. In a sweeping motion, she swung both swords through their throats simultaneously. This left only The Apprentice, who was shaking with fear.

"*Come on little man, give me your best shot.*" The Apprentice didn't move, as if paralyzed. Jamie only egged him on again.

"*What's the matter, gonna wet yourself?*" That alone drew his ire, brandishing two knives from his belt. He charged at her with reckless abandon. Jamie targeted his genitals, abruptly piercing his balls with her swords. The pain was extraordinary, but she wasn't done. Methodically, she ripped downward as blood rained to the ground. Not satisfied at all, she tore off his dick.

"*Ahhhhhhhhhhhhhhh*" He screamed out in the air.

"*Scream!! Scream mother fucker!!*" She was utterly ruthless. Down to his knees, he pressed his hands against the wound, trying in vain to stop the bleeding. In response, she slowly pushed her swords through his stomach. He gurgled in shock as blood gushed down his mouth. She looked him dead in the eyes and spoke with venom.

"*For Raven.*" In unfathomable fury, she ripped out her swords from his stomach, crossed both blades at his throat, and viciously closed the gap, severing his head completely. Jamie spit on his face before walking away, her mission complete.

Part VII: Riker

Rain fell from the sky. The droplets turned to blood as strings of fire rose up from the ground. In the background stood old, decrepit structures wrapped in chains. The hollow faced demons reemerged in front of him. They whispered venomous inclinations as the poison grew more potent in Ray's mind. There seemed to be no end in sight. Ray desperately tried to fight their words, with hope quickly fleeting. He could not endure another setback. At that moment, he opened his eyes to reality. Strangely, he was not confined to a cell. In fact, he was alone in the darkness, facing an empty hallway. He was defenseless as he walked patiently toward the exit, his eyes blind to unforeseen threats. Yet, none came forth to stop him. He felt uneasy, and kept a steady breath. As he came closer to the large double doors in front of him, he heard shouts of pain and gasps of air that might have been from sex. Bracing himself, he slowly opened the doors to madness. He could see them all. Mai was strung upside down off a tree branch. She hung there, stripped down to her underwear with a noticeable puncture wound in her side. She grew extremely weak. If that wasn't enough, Avery Jackson was tied up to another tree, bruised and bloody after taking multiple shots to the face with his own brass knuckles. He then witnessed a sledgehammer careen into his stomach, causing blood to spew from his mouth. His torturers laughed uproariously, sending disdain through Riker's eyes. As he shifted his eyes to the right, he saw a final image. It was his own daughter, stripped nude, her face battered. The sight alone burned his veins, but what he saw next was completely detestable. He could see the cretin kneel down and penetrate her, violently throttling her body, over and over again. The faint screams infecting his heart. Desmond Reaper was standing in a half circle of flame in the distance, taunting him.

Suddenly, at that moment, Riker found himself gasping for air. He felt the beast inside tear and rip and claw towards his heart. Electricity began to spark in his mind all around him. Rage intensified with every short breath as the demon eagerly anticipated his release. Poison ash began to flow deeply into his lungs until it tunneled through every molecule in his body, spreading like the plague. Darkness utterly consumed him. His tears became like blood and his eyes reeked of brimstone. He could not control himself any longer and felt nothing but the burning desire to kill. At that moment, so overwhelmed with hate, his eyes began to roll towards the back of his head. Within seconds he collapsed to the ground. In his dreamworld he entered a place he had never seen before. The earth became like coal and the sky turned to flame. Large structures resembling medieval castles lay in ruin at the forefront. The gates surrounding him appeared rusty and stale.

I could hear the voices of children in the background and found myself surrounded by their ghosts. Just then, a blinding light seeped through my eyes and I found myself frozen, unable to move. From the ashes he rose from the surface. His red eyes glared at mine with unsurpassed intensity. A black cloud of smoke circled around him. He raised his hand and pulled me towards him. What madness was this? Everything seemed so real. Satan himself lured me into his fortress, trapping me like an insect struggling to survive in the spider's web. The smell of fire and brimstone engulfed my very surroundings. Suddenly, I could feel my throat begin to tighten as my lungs filled with the noxious fumes of blackened ash. Death seemed eminent, but at the last second he released his grip on me. I violently fell to the ground. What happened next was rather unexpected. I felt a woman's touch on my chest and this kiss on my neck. When I looked up I saw yet another coming toward me. She slowly began to remove her silk blouse and started groping my chest. She proceeded to lick my neck and cheek. Her eyes were a crimson red and her saliva was sweet like honey. I knew what was happening. It was the seduction of the contract. My mind was torn down the middle with no sense of rationality. In the background I could hear the demon laughing. Motivating me even further the women merged together, transforming into the Greek goddess Aphrodite if I ever saw her. She grabbed my face with both hands and revealed her serpent tipped tongue. It was the kiss to seal the deal, to forever bind with true evil. As she went to make her move I closed my eyes to give in to the demon's contract. Then again, why would I give in to that piece of shit? Did he actually think his attempt to control me would work? How pathetic he became. I am my own devil, free to do whatever the fuck I want. My mission is to exterminate the scum who walk the earth, preying on the innocent. When I opened my eyes I grabbed the bitches' throat, formed a sword with my hand and thrust it into her soulless heart. Her scream was music to my ears. Before administrating the final blow I looked directly at the devil and yelled. "Fuck you!" I pulled the sword out of her heart and sliced her head off.

"*You tell your minions. I bow down to no one!*" With those emphatic words I was struck by two sets of lightning bolts and blacked out. Before I faded to dark I remembered seeing my reflection in the mirror. My eyes were dark blue. I awoke again, only to find myself trapped in another hell. No, what is this? I saw fire, the earth was on fire but this was different. The fire turned red as if mixed with blood. Everything was gone, there was nothing left.

"*Ahhhhhhhhhhhhhhhhhhh*" I screamed in my mind. Everything was engulfed in the flames of chaos, anarchy, and despair. I closed my eyes, then opened them, but nothing changed. From out of nowhere I felt excruciating pain, like knives pressing tightly in my ears. With fire surrounding me I saw them all, every single person I cared about. Just then, I looked down at my hands and an overwhelming sense of hysteria took over me. I couldn't control this sensation pulsating through my veins, and the most horrifying thing was, I enjoyed it. I embraced the uncontrollable rage within. I basked in the power, the greed, and the lust of its very essence. I became fixated on it, but as though a warning was sent, my loved ones reappeared in front of me. This time, however, I saw fear in their eyes. Within seconds I found myself pulling out my gun and firing without mercy, without control. I tried to stop myself with everything deep inside of me but to no avail. I no longer had control of my body. I could only watch in terror as I killed them all, every single one. Tears of blood rolled down my cheeks. Why was this happening? Get me out of this hell. My head was about to explode.

"Get me oooooouuuuuuuuut!!!!!!!" No matter how hard I screamed I remained trapped in this place, trapped in this rage I could not stop. It was constant, never ending. My eyes opened, cold, devoid of substance, as if hollow inside. This was reality, and it was clear. I knew what I had to do. Several men slowly converged on Riker. Before they got within his range, Jamie O'Neil came out of the shadows and joined Riker by his side. She looked at Riker and handed him a sword.

"I come bearing a gift." She said as she readied her stance.

Riker didn't look at her when he took it, just stood there, his eyes locked on Reaper.

"Do whatever you want, but Reaper belongs to me." That is when the beast let out. Riker immediately stepped into the fray. He thrust forward and slashed the first man through his stomach and cut off his head. Blood soaked his face. As another came forward, Riker pivoted to his right and with both hands gripping his sword, cut through his throat. Immediately, he launched himself in the air and ripped through the next victim, tearing him in half. A more formidable opponent was in front of him, armed with a sword as well. He swung diagonally towards him, but blocked down low, then met him up high. The steel glistened erratically with each blow. When Riker blocked the next attack at the midsection,

he found an opening and kicked him in the stomach, sending him to the ground.

He offered his opponent the respect of allowing him to get back up for round two. Again and again, blades connected with each other, rattling and rocketing with each brutal blow. As he blocked an attack to his right, he kicked him in the groin, dropping him to his knees. He then aggressively chopped off his left arm, before turning the blade sideways and skewering his neck. While this was in progress, Jamie headed toward Avery and found herself facing a man armed with an axe. Before he could react, she slid down and sliced off his ankle. She then bounced back up and severed his head, blood erupting in her face. She grabbed hold of the axe and tossed it to Riker. Placing the sword behind his belt, he wielded the axe with lethal precision. He violently swung it against the next one's stomach, gushing out drops of blood. He ripped the axe from his stomach and saw him crouched over. The axe raised up and crashed down multiple times on his neck, severing his head completely. The demon then launched the axe and watched it spin directly into the next man's chest.

Jamie slashed a man diagonally up his chest before savagely dragging the blade down his opposite side, dismembering most of his torso. She moved intently toward Avery and cut him free. Following suit, she cut down Mai as well. As this was happening, Riker rearmed himself with the sword and sent it through a man's chest, twisting it as he did. Afterward, he ripped it out and slit his throat. Avery, too weak to fight, took hold of the sledgehammer on the ground. As Riker began to close in on Lisa's location, Avery caught his attention.

"*Riker!*" Avery tossed him the sledgehammer. As he took hold of it, he dropped the sword to the ground. Three men stood in the way of Lisa, while another continued to penetrate her. Riker barreled toward them, tightening his grip on the sledgehammer. In his madness he let loose a sickening barrage. He cocked back the weapon and drove it against the man's face. Instantaneously, he thrust the hammer against the next one's stomach and brutally reigned it down upon his head. The force crippled his skull. Afterward, he jabbed the next man in the chest with the handle before ramming the hammer up against his jaw. He followed that up with a vicious strike, sending the hammer diagonally down his face. He then rushed at the man raping Lisa and wrapped the handle around his neck, dragging him off her. As he was down, Riker sent the hammer crashing down on his groin. He wailed in agony from the effect. Riker then winded back the hammer and struck the man's face as hard as he could, shredding skin and bone. He was not finished. Again and again, the hammer rattled the man's brain, turning it to mulch as blood sprayed everywhere. There was no mercy to be had. Finally it was over.

Riker knelt down, removed his shirt, and placed it over his daughter as she wept. Looking around, there was no one left, only Reaper. The monster was smiling at him.

Jamie finished off the last of his minions, ripping the blade from his eye. His chainsaw was still humming on the ground. This intrigued Jamie. She picked up the fallen weapon and walked over to Riker, who was staring a hole through Reaper's eyes. Not saying a word, Riker dropped the sledgehammer as he was given the chainsaw by Jamie.

"Remember what I said earlier? Forget all of it, I won't stop you." Said Jamie.

The stage was set for the final confrontation. Reaper merely stood there provoking him, with that same sadistic smile. At that moment, Riker walked toward his judgement day, the chainsaw growling as he stepped closer. The heat from the flames fueled his hatred. Before Reaper could speak, Riker sliced the chainsaw through Reaper's stomach, tearing out his back. He collapsed down to the ground. With pure animosity, Riker pulled out the saw and aimed it directly at Reaper's face, the saw letting out an evil hissing sound. Reaper looked into the eyes of his executioner and saw nothing but darkness bathed in red.

"*You lose.*" Riker whispered before ramming the saw through Reaper's mouth, blood splashing against his face. They were all dead. I dropped down to my knees, drenched in blood. We stood together, taking in the moment as the flames continued to burn. I then turned my attention back to Lisa and kissed her on the forehead.

"You're OK honey, I'm here."

Avery brought Mai over to them.

"How's she doing?" I asked.

"She's still breathing, but we need to get her to a hospital. You know how to fly a plane?"

"I do." Jamie said.

"Good, let's get the hell out of here."

"No, not yet. We must rid ourselves of this place once and for all."

"What are you thinking Ray?" asked Avery.

"Did you bring the detonator?"

"Yeah."

"Burn it, burn it all." They watched the flames burn from the plane above. Lisa rested her head on her father's shoulder. He kissed her on the forehead before gazing out the window. In the horizon, he could see the sun begin to rise. Peace swept over him as could see his wife's face embedded in the clouds.

Printed in the United States
by Baker & Taylor Publisher Services